Double Sunset

Kristin Smith

Susan,
I love working
with you!
Happy reading!
Kristin

Strangers

by: Mark Turbyfill (1896-1991)

I shall tell you:

I am seeing and seeing strangers

Who are not strangers,

For there is something in their eyes,

And about their faces

That whispers to me

(But so low

That I can never quite hear)

Of the lost half of myself

Which I have been seeking since the beginning of earth;

And I could follow them to the end of the world,

Would they but lean nearer, nearer,

And tell me....

Chapter 1

Almost as if being dropped from above, I landed in a soft, prickly pile of hay. All around me the pungent, damp smell of animals, manure, rust, and wood accosted my senses. Bracing myself the best I could I rolled out of the hay pile, surveying my surroundings.

I was in a very old barn that should have long since buckled under the years it had stood. Instead, it was vibrant with activity. I could hear the animals below me, bickering out their morning annoyances. The sunlight filtered in through the high windows and laid long dusty lines across the hay-littered floor.

Brushing the hay from my clothes, I was acutely aware of the long petticoat and red checkered skirt that hung over brown boots. The apron I was wearing over the skirt and blouse had hay clinging desperately to every thread. I caught sight of a long piece of hay dangling from my brown hair, inching closer into my line of vision. Plucking it and allowing several others to follow to the floor, I scanned the room again, looking for something I recognized.

There was a wooden ladder clinging to the wood a few feet from me. It led to the dusty, hay splattered floor below. Hiking up my skirt in my arms, I descended from the second floor. Pushing away from the ladder, I let my full skirt fall back around my legs.

As I looked up, there was a horse staring right at me, its long lashes blinking a hello. I walked over to the pen and gently patted the long nose of the most gorgeous creature I had ever seen. It was chocolaty brown with a long, white stripe going down its nose and winding around each nostril, which opened and closed as if it were taking in my scent. As I was patting the horse, a few chickens sauntered into the open space, the light coming through the massive doorway lighting up their stage as they pecked about, chattering and clucking to each other. This made me chuckle as I moved toward the door to take in the outside.

Just as I approached the doorway, I saw three figures in the distance. I crouched beside the door so as not to be discovered; something told me I shouldn't be here. The three were walking toward the barn. Each had a basket on their arms. As they got closer, I could begin to hear their banter.

"Katherine, I want to get the biggest one today. Mama said that it was my turn to bring her the biggest egg."

"I'm the only boy, so I should get the biggest egg," he boasted, puffing out his chest, shoving a bit of dust at the little girl with his boot, and making her pout and grab at the tall girl's apron.

"That's enough out of both of you. Let's make it a game. After we gather all of the eggs, we will hide them and then play a game of Find the Eggs. Whoever finds the most gets to give Mama the biggest one." The tall girl ruffled the little girl's hair and glowered at the boy.

"Oh Katherine, that sounds like fun, but what if one of the eggs breaks? Pa will be real sore, he will probably…" And she was cut off by Katherine's scolding glare.

I could just make out the worry lines across the girl's forehead as the three came closer to the doorway. I moved farther along the wall, behind a pile of hay so they wouldn't see me. The three entered the barn and made their way to the back wall, just out of my view. They exited the other side and made their way to the small chicken coop just beyond the barn. I could barely hear their voices as they gathered the eggs. I couldn't make out what they were saying, but it sounded like the little girl was singing, something I had never heard before but I knew every word.

I stayed behind the hay pile, waiting for their return. As their voices grew louder and more distinct, I peeked out from behind the pile and caught a glimpse of the three coming back through the barn, the boy hanging back, dragging a stick through the dirt, sending plumes of dry gray fog into the air around his legs.

"*OK, so here is how it works. Gabriel, you take that side of the barn.*" *She was pointing right where I stood.* "*Becca, you can take this part of the barn over here, and I will take that area over there. We hide our eggs, and Gabe, remember your sister is just five. Then we find them, only we can't look in the area where we hid ours. We each have six eggs to hide, Gabe, how many does that make in all?*"

"*Oh, come on Katherine, don't make me do arithmetic.*"

Gabe started walking over toward me. I was going to be found. I crouched down behind the pile, hoping he would decide it was not a good hiding spot. I could hear Becca's giggles as Katherine called to her to make sure she was hiding them well.

I liked this girl. She was strong and obviously loved her brother and sister very much. I felt drawn to her and wished that I had chosen her side as my hiding place so that she would find me instead of Gabriel.

Just as I was thinking this, I heard his boots clomping on the floor right near me. He came into view, his back to me, as he hid an egg in a small bucket that sat in the corner. When he turns around he will see me crouched on the floor, I thought, my arms wrapped around my knees trying to be invisible.

He looked around, trying to find another hiding spot, a brown egg perched in his hand. Almost as if in slow motion, he turned to face me, his eyes darting around the small area. They never came to rest on me. Couldn't he see me? He walked over to the hay pile, standing just inches away. His boots were almost touching the tips of mine as he carefully placed an egg in the hay, inches from my face. He looked at it for a minute, making sure it wouldn't sink deeper into the pile and be hidden. Then he turned and ran back into the center of the barn. He hadn't seen me! Was I really invisible?

All three reconvened in the center of the barn and waited for Katherine to send them on their search. Katherine sent them on their way while she headed right in my direction. I stood up and moved a few inches out from the pile, wondering if she would be able to see me. My boots making noise on the creaky wooden floor, I crept out from behind the hay pile. By this time, she was walking straight for me, her eyes scanning the surroundings but, like her brother, not landing on me.

She was beautiful, and I couldn't take my eyes off of her. She looked oddly familiar; like her chocolate eyes had belonged to someone I used to know. Her long, brown hair was braided down her back. She was almost upon me when I noticed that she wore the exact same outfit that I was wearing.

Katherine moved right by me, her shoulder almost brushing mine as she spied the egg in the barrel. After she found the egg in the hay pile, I followed her back to the center of the barn where Becca was standing, examining her eggs. Gabe was nowhere in sight and I saw Katherine drop two of her eggs into Becca's basket with a wink and a finger to her lips. Becca fought to stifle a giggle as Gabe skidded to a stop in front of them.

"OK, let's count." Gabe set his basket on the floor and plopped down next to it, sending hay and dust all around him.

"Let Becca do the counting," Katherine chided.

"I have the most." Becca grabbed the biggest one out of Gabe's basket and ran out the door yelling, "Mama, look what I have for you!"

Katherine extended a hand to Gabe to pull him up off the ground. He swatted at her hand like it was a fly and hoisted himself up off the dusty barn floor.

"Thank you, Gabe, for not making a stink for Becca's sake." She smiled at her brother who stuck his tongue out in return.

"Come on, I'll race you back." Gabe gently pushed Katherine as he started for the door. Katherine leaned down and gently moved all the eggs into her basket and, shaking her head, walked out the large doorway into the sunlight.

I was mesmerized by this scene. It was so familiar to me, yet foreign at the same time. Almost without realizing it, I followed them out of the barn into the bright sunlight. The light blinded me, and I raised my arm to shield them as the ground began to spiral and the dust began to swirl up from my feet and engulf me in its wake.

The dream hung with me all morning as I went about getting ready for the day. I had a hard time shaking it. I could see each of the three children's faces: Katherine's natural beauty, Becca's bright laughing face, and Gabriel's sadness hidden by his hard exterior. They felt so familiar in an odd way, as if I knew their life's story but couldn't conjure it up. It was just out of reach.

I don't think I had ever had a dream quite like this one; it was so real that it felt as if a part of it was still playing out in my heart. It left a strange feeling with me, as if a small seed had been planted and was taking root. I tried to shake it off as I got ready for the day, but like the smell of a bonfire, it seemed to linger on my clothes and in my mind all morning, and I wasn't sure I liked it.

I looked at the little alarm clock that sat on the faded kitchen counter, barely registering the time: 11:17. I decided I needed to get some groceries and start cooking and settle in. I had been in my new home for two days now and was more than ready to explore my surroundings. My stomach grumbled under my shirt reminding me that food was most important right now. Aunt Cathy, bless her heart, had the groundskeepers leave some food in the refrigerator as well as a beautiful bouquet of flowers that greeted me happily from the kitchen table.

I knew there was a little market at the end of the road; it would be a long walk but certainly not impossible. I saw a bike under the back steps which had a nice, large basket in the front. Winding my long, brown hair into a bun on top of my head, I grabbed the bike and pushed it up the hill to the top of the lane. It had been a long time since I rode a bike, but as I started down Reacliffe Road toward the market, I marveled at how easily it all came back.

The day was beautiful, couldn't have been more perfect. Not a cloud in the sky, birds chirping in their nests as they wait for their morning meal. I felt like chirping myself as I climbed on the bike and started down the lane. Then it dawned on me that this was the first time I had felt somewhat content and happy since I left the States. I suddenly felt guilty but pushed that thought right back out of my mind. This was my new life, and I had to embrace it; it's what my mom would want me to do.

"Bloom where you're planted," Mom always said. It was her way of reminding us that life doesn't always give us what we want, but we need to embrace what it does give us and make the best of it. It was how Mom lived her life and was one of the greatest lessons she taught me. However, I had been struggling to find out how to apply this to my life now, but Mom kept whispering in my ear, "Bloom where you're planted, Ava."

The last two nights had been difficult; I was alone in a new place and really wasn't sure what I was doing here. It had seemed like a good idea when I was safe at home in North Carolina. Now, 3000 miles away, I wasn't sure anymore.

"Ava, you haven't been yourself for awhile," I could hear Aunt Cathy say. She was right. I wasn't sure if I would ever be myself again. Sometimes life changes you.

The cloudless sky and beautiful sun forced me to put that out of my head for the time being. The ride down the lane was pleasant; the stone walls on either side of the road propelled me forward and gave me a nice sense of security. As I rode I thought about Aunt Cathy and Uncle Bern, the only family I had left. They would be in their huge North Carolina home waiting to hear from me and ready to offer anything they could to me, their "adopted" daughter.

They never had any children and had always done whatever they could to help me and my mom. They were the closest thing to parents I had now. Aunt Cathy was the sweetest woman I knew. She worked at the local library, helping people find just the book they needed, which was the perfect job for someone who always did everything for everyone. She didn't have to work; Uncle Bern made enough money at his job as an engineer, and he had come from "family money" that set them up for the rest of their lives. They worked to keep busy. I had known them all my life; they had helped to raise me. Mom and I had lived in their basement apartment until I was 5.

It was only natural that they would have offered me their lake cottage for the summer, but I still wasn't sure what I was doing here. Was I running away, or was I really trying to figure out how I was going to get through the rest of my life? A train whistle blared in the distance as if it was answering my question.

The little market was at the bottom of the lane right before the bend in the road that leads to the docks and the public access to the lake. I found a spot for the bike and leaned it carefully against the building and turned to face the small cottage. It looked like it had once been a house but now had a sign hung over the door that read "Hollings Market." As I approached the door, the smell of cinnamon and sugar snuck out of the open window, and it made me stop short as I remembered this scent from my childhood.

My mom would make cookies as gifts for Christmas, and our house smelled like cinnamon and sugar from October through December. The smell paralyzed me for a minute as I was transported back to the comfort of my mom and my perfect childhood in North Carolina. For just a moment I wasn't sure what to do. Move forward? Turn around and run? But to where? Keep moving forward was all I could do, what my mom would want me to do.

Tears pricking at the back of my throat, I quickly opened the door, barely noticing the tiny tinkling of the bell that announced my arrival. The smell doubled in intensity as I took in a deep breath and let it cleanse me anew. Embrace it, I told myself. Create new memories where old ones lingered.

My eyes surveyed the surroundings, trying to decide where to settle; there was so much to take in. I noticed a small counter by the door with an old time register, five or six rows of groceries, and far in the back what looked like a bakery. This must be where the smell was coming from. Feeling as if I had stepped into the past in this humble little place, I immediately liked the way it made me feel.

A woman's voice, lyrical, almost like she was singing, found my ears. She was talking to someone, laughing. I knew instantly I liked this woman, and her English accent propelled me forward. My legs took me down one of the aisles, to the place where my childhood smells and this new laughter mixed. At the end of the aisle, I stopped short.

There in front of me was a long counter of the most delicious baked goods I had ever seen. Behind the counter was a woman, her back to me, a long braid down her back. From this angle I couldn't tell her age, but she was slightly round with age and her stance showed an air of purpose, of many years of hard work, determination and grit. She was talking to someone that was just out of my eyesight, around the corner. She was telling a story about a cat that had appeared on her doorstep earlier that morning. It didn't matter what she was saying; her voice was mesmerizing, and I just wanted to stay in this moment for a little while longer.

A little noise escaped my lips, and the woman turned slowly to look at me. She appeared to be mid-forties, beautiful, in a life-well-lived kind of way. Her blue eyes blinked softly in my direction as her smile lit up her fresh, natural face. She fit into this little space as if she were built out of the stone, sugary smells, and stories that made up this curious little store.

"Oh dear, hello there," she said in her musical voice and obvious English accent.

It took me a minute to find my voice. "Hello." I felt like I was intruding and I shouldn't be there. "I'm Ava," I said, almost as a question. "I'm staying out on the lake in the Murphy's cottage for the summer."

"Welcome to Rudyard Lake, Ava. It is nice to have a new face around here. I am Elise Hollings. My husband, James, and I own this little piece of heaven." She giggled as if remembering a joke.

Instantly, I wanted to know everything there was to know about this couple, this lake, and this tiny market. From around the corner emerged a man, rather short, somewhat round, and appropriately balding. He seemed to be a little older than Elise and looked worn but had friendliness in his deep set green eyes. There was an air of familiarity to him, like I had met him before. He didn't say anything, but nodded in introduction as he wiped his hands on his apron. I knew at once that he had been around the corner making whatever smelled so appealing, and for this I liked him instantly.

"What can we get for you, dear? We don't have everything here, but we hope to have what you need," said Elise. How profound her statement sounded to me.

"Well, I've only been here two days, and I would like to get some things for the cottage."

Elise guided me through the aisles as she and I both slipped things into the baskets we each held. She chattered on about the lake, the market, and even the weather. I hardly noticed her words but was comforted by the melody of her voice and her lyrical accent.

When we had gathered all that we could, we started up toward the register. After ringing up and bagging my items, Elise called toward the back, "James, bring up some rolls for Ava, please." She added four cinnamon buns to my bag and told me to enjoy them. I wanted to hug her but realized this would be a bit awkward seeing as how we just met. Thanking her, I turned toward the door, announcing that I would be back soon. Her smile warmed me as I crossed out into the sunlight.

Stepping out of the market with four bags, I instantly realized that they would not fit in the bike basket. I had been so preoccupied, almost in a trance, as I navigated the aisles with Elise that I hadn't even thought about getting my bags back to the cottage.

Now what to do? I put two bags in the basket, all that would fit, and hung the other two from the handlebars. As I straddled the bike and tried to get it moving, the front bars twisted and turned under the weight, and I knew this was not going to work. I stepped off the bike and contemplated walking back; I would have to come retrieve it later.

Just as I removed the bags from the bars, I heard the crunching of pebbles behind me. I turned to see a boy about my age. He was leaning against the rock wall by the road with a look of almost amusement on his face. His arms were folded in front of him as he appraised me.

How long had he been standing there? My face blushed in embarrassment. We looked at each other for a long time. Something inside me was stirring; it almost felt like it was trying to wake up- a feeling I had never felt before but at the same time felt completely natural. It was difficult to ignore the thoughts bouncing off the inside of my brain, like crashing waves on the shore. I tried, unsuccessfully, to grasp onto one thought as they sloshed about.

This boy was tall and thin with the faint traces of muscle under his shirt. He looked to be right on the edge of manhood, but not quite there yet. He appeared to be somewhat wet, like he had not long been out of the shower, or perhaps the lake. His deep, green eyes watched me as a few strands of hair fell from my bun across my eyes.

Finally he spoke. "Need some help?" He held a smug look on his face as if he was finding amusement in my predicament. My heart quickened, an oddly familiar feeling, similar to how I felt when I saw James. This boy had to be their son; he looked like a perfect combination of both James and Elise.

I wasn't sure what to say as the blush began to rise on my cheeks. Without much thought, I blurted out, "Yes, that would be lovely, thank you. I am Ava, and I am staying out on the lake, at the end of Pine Lane."

"Jack Hollings, nice to meet you, Ava."

His eyes were laughing as he hopped down the small slanted path. I was a little irritated at his amusement and wished I could just dump the bags and ride back to the safety of the cottage where I could stop my heart from racing.

He grabbed the bike as I adjusted the two bags in my hands. He started down the lane, pushing the bike with ease. It was clear he meant to walk me, the groceries, and the bike home. As comforting as this whole scene was, it was too new to be familiar, and I had to keep reminding myself that I didn't know this person and was still mildly annoyed at his air of presumptuousness.

We walked a few moments in silence. I had no idea what to say, but the silence was not hard; it was comforting, like I had made this walk a hundred times with him. It also helped to slow my heartbeat and quiet my thoughts. I kept glancing up at his face trying to figure out this growing feeling of comfort and peace that I had as we walked. Something very deep inside of me was trying to tell me that I knew this boy, but I kept fighting it back down. The absurdity of it all was making me feel lightheaded.

Finally he spoke, and I instantly noticed his British drawl, and it filled me with comfort- there was something about a British accent that made me want to giggle and curl up in a warm blanket at the same time.

"So where in the states are you from, Ava?"

"Just outside of Charlotte, North Carolina."

"And what brings you to Rudyard Lake?"

This question brought me to a stop. The memories flooded back; can I tell him everything? I was feeling very protective of my pain and wasn't ready to spill it out. I started walking again and had to do a double step to catch up. He had kept walking, almost oblivious to my brief lapse.

"My aunt and uncle own the cottage and are letting me stay here for the summer before I start college in the fall." This was true, I had not lied, although I wouldn't be starting college in the fall; this only I knew. I hadn't bothered to tell Aunt Cathy and Uncle Bern that I never returned my acceptance letter.

Memories of the past winter started to flood, and I quickly looked at Jack's face to bring me back to reality. He had a defined jaw bone and happy eyes, as if he found amusement in everything. At first they appeared to be blue, but then I noticed some specks of green, and they almost seemed to transform before my own dull brown eyes. His brown hair was wavy and hung over his ears in a very unruly way, carefree. Full lips held a purpose for his face, almost positioned in a permanent grin. He was ruggedly good looking, as if he had lived his life outdoors. His features were very defined but the happiness in his green eyes softened them. His wavy, brown hair looked as if he just ran his fingers through it because he couldn't be bothered with it. It suited him well and overall he was very good-looking. I had to stop my thoughts and focus on what he was saying.

"Well, it will be nice to have a new face around here. Do you canoe?"

"Um, no I have never been on a canoe; don't think it is my thing."

"That's a shame, I am thinking about starting a canoeing class down at the sailing club. I teach classes down there throughout the year. Swimming, boating, fishing, you name it."

"That sounds like a fun job." I pulled this out, not wanting to let him know how horrifying that really sounded to me. I had never liked the water. Even though my mom had always meant to, she had never signed me up for formal swimming lessons. Aunt Cathy tried once to teach me, but my fear of the water was already so deep that the farthest I would allow her to take me into the pool was to my knees.

We still had a little ways to walk, and while I was aware of Jack's prattle going on beside me, I was having too much trouble focusing on what he was saying. My mind was drifting all over the place, from the gorgeous scenery around me to the high-pitched swaying song of the birds above. If I concentrated, I could hear them having a conversation. When I was little, I used to sit outside and make up those conversations in my head, what one bird was saying to the other and the responses he received. I've never been very good at conversation, but with the birds I could've made them up all day. This is probably why I was having trouble keeping up with Jack's exchange. I had to force myself to concentrate on what he was saying.

"In 1863, John Kipling and Alice Macdonald found love right here on Rudyard Lake. They loved this place so much that they named their first son after the lake."

When he looked at me to see if I understood what he was saying, I guess the look on my face was confusion, and he continued, "Rudyard Kipling." He laughed a bit as he said it.

I nodded to show him that I knew who he meant, the famous English poet, but my thoughts were all over the place. They were a pebble skipping out over the lake, each ripple of thought joining another and spiraling outward, just out of my grasp. My focus was all askew; my mom used to say I was "jumbling" whenever I had trouble putting my thoughts together. I was definitely "jumbling" now. I shook my head and forced myself to focus on Jack and this walk.

I couldn't believe we were already at the top of Pine Lane. I stopped and offered to take the bags the rest of the way, just 100 yards down the steep slope of asphalt into the wilderness and the lake beyond.

"I don't mind walking them all the way, unless you don't want me to see where you live?" he said with a little nudge of my shoulder.

Oddly, I wasn't ready for him to leave. I couldn't explain it myself if I tried, but a part of me didn't want him to ever leave.

Slightly annoyed at myself, I just began walking and saw that he was following. About halfway down the lane, I turned to him. "Thank you for offering to walk me home, I really appreciate it."

"Not a problem, I love walking the lake. Although this area I am really unfamiliar with; I don't think I have ever ventured off Reacliffe Road in this direction." I could tell that he was admiring the trees and depth of the woods around us.

My cottage was at the very end, right on the lake. It was the only house in this immediate area. I had neighbors, but you had to walk through the woods on either side to get to them. The calm feeling of seclusion it provided was just what I needed.

The cottage was mostly stone with a few patches of painted white wood. It looked as if whoever built it didn't have enough stone to finish it, so they threw in some wood here and there to complete it. Basically five rooms made up the home. The first floor consisted of a kitchen and living room that had been opened up so that it appeared to be one large room. The far wall was mostly windows. The double glass doors opened out to the patio, small patch of grass, and then the lake. The large picture window stood to the side of the patio door and offered more views of the lake. The second floor held two small bedrooms and a bathroom. It was a small, cozy cottage that seemed to have a life of its own.

"My uncle has had this in his family for years; I think maybe his great-grandparents built it? I used to come over with my mom when I was little, but I don't really remember."

Oh, that was hard to get out. I stopped short after that, and all of a sudden I didn't want to tell him anything more about my past. Fortunately, he didn't ask any questions as we veered off the road onto the cottage path. It was part dirt, part stone, which looked like it had been crafted by someone who drank too much the way it meandered from the lane to the cottage door.

I hesitated a minute at the door, unsure if I should invite him in or take the bags and say our goodbyes. Too quickly, I unlocked the door and ushered him in. The kitchen is tiny, but Uncle Bern had opened up half of the far wall that looks into the living room and out over the lake. It made for perfect views from anywhere.

He put the bags on the counter and turned to look at me. It was weird; I felt strangely drawn to him, and I didn't want him to leave. It was strange because I had this feeling that he was thinking the same thing. I wasn't sure I liked it but felt powerless to stop it. I quickly pulled my hair tighter into the bun so the few strands that had escaped were now neatly put back into place where they belonged.

"Would you like to see the lake from here?" I turned and started for the living room and the double doors that opened to the patio and lake. When we walked out on the patio, the weather's perfection and the sweet breeze coming off the lake hit us both, and we each took in a deep breath. The day's weather was absolutely picture perfect. The sharp smell of the lake was strangely pleasing, similar to a good cup of strong coffee.

We both sat down on the porch swing at almost the same time, sending it rocking back and almost dumping us both back onto the patio. We grabbed the sides and steadied it as we busted out laughing.

I already knew that Jack Hollings was going to be a great person for me to know on this lake, and the thought of being around his mother again made me smile. I couldn't process the feelings I was having; it had been so long since I felt anything even close to happiness or contentment. It felt strangely familiar yet completely foreign at the same time.

I also couldn't explain the feelings I was having for Jack. How could I feel so comfortable with someone I had just met? I was trying to push away just how attracted I was to him and remember why I had come to the lake. I watched him admiring the lake, his green eyes scanning over the surroundings. I loved how his wavy brown hair hung in his eyes, and I had to constantly stifle the urge to push those strands away.

"I don't think you can get a better view from anywhere else on this lake." Jack seemed completely mesmerized by the lake and hills beyond it. It was breathtaking, and I liked sharing it with him, knowing that he lived here and seemed to have never noticed the lake's beauty before today. In silence we both looked across the lake to the dense green trees and hills that were just barely visible above the tree line. Jack's eyes darted around the lake taking in every sight, his smile never leaving his face. The green in his eyes seemed to deepen with the green of the trees surrounding us.

"Do you ever hike around here?" I blurted out.

"Sure do, but the best trails are on the other side, so the easiest way over is to canoe. I will be sure to plan a trip and take you along really soon. Sometimes on Saturdays I will take a group out that wants to see the sights." He reached over and plucked a leaf off of my jacket, throwing it over the back of the swing.

I am not sure why I blushed, but this was enough to force me off the swing. Hopping off, I headed back into the kitchen to put away the groceries. Expecting Jack to follow me, I turned around in the kitchen and caught his profile on the patio, still looking out over the lake.

He stood like that for a long time, and I stood in the kitchen watching him watch the lake. The way he stood and carried himself was way beyond his years, as if he possessed an old soul. Yet he was also childishly carefree; it was an odd combination. Shaking my head, I turned to the bags on the counter muttering to myself, "Stay focused, Ava."

Jack walked slowly back into the kitchen, he looked deep in thought. A few more strands of hair fell lose around my face, and for a minute I thought he was going to brush them back. Quickly, I tucked them behind my ears and turned away from him.

"I like how your eyes and your hair are almost the exact same shade of brown." I turned to see Jack leaning against the counter watching me. Our eyes met for a second, and for once he was the first to look away, but not before I noticed his smile widen.

"Well, I think I'd better get these groceries unpacked. I appreciate your help." I straightened my back and began to unload the bags.

Jack said his goodbyes and told me he would be by to check on me sometime during the week. He left me his home and cell numbers if I needed anything. I was rolling my eyes at him by the time I pushed him out the back door and watched him jog up the hill. The breeze carried with it a tune Jack was whistling that I thought I had heard before but couldn't place where. It filled me with a strange feeling of nostalgia and serenity.

I turned on some music while I put away the groceries. I wanted to set up all of my painting equipment in the living room so that I could maybe squeak in a few hours of painting before the sun went down. One of the many reasons that Aunt Cathy wanted me to come to Rudyard Lake this summer was for my painting. She was right about one thing- the scenery around here was breathtaking. Aunt Cathy also knew that my painting was very healing for me, and I needed to grieve and heal which I had been unable to do in North Carolina.

I tried to push my mom out of my head; I wasn't sure that I was ready for those emotions again. But as I was learning, grief was a wave, gentling stirring under the calm water's surface.

Without warning, the wave would build, and once it started there was nothing stopping it until it reached shore and seeped back into the tiny cracks and crevices of life.

I could feel the tears start to well, so I stopped in the kitchen and found my way to the living room couch where I allowed myself to cry. Cry for my mother who died so young in such a senseless way. I cried for myself, now 18 and without my mother, alone in an unfamiliar place trying to put my life's broken pieces back together.

I could remember my conversation with Aunt Cathy like it was happening in front of me.

"Ava, you know how much Bernie and I adore you?" she began. "We would do anything for you, you know that. Well, I have been doing some thinking." She hesitated and watched my face for any sign of a reaction, which I didn't give to her. My emotions lately had been numb, my moods surly. The day my mother died, a large part of me died right with her, and I no longer knew how to live.

She chose her words carefully. "Your uncle and I think that it might be nice for you to spend some time away, clear your head and grieve." When I didn't respond, she continued, "You remember your uncle's cottage on Rudyard Lake?"

I nodded and let her continue.

"Well, we would like to offer it to you for the summer. It is truly a magical place, it's…" and then she stopped, deciding her words may not be the best at the moment.

I tried to pretend that I didn't know what she was going to say. She and Uncle Bern had met and fallen in love there. It was a truly magical place for them. I have never met two people so absolutely in tune with each other and still very much in love after 24 years. I had always marveled at their love, knowing it was something extremely rare. I had never tired of hearing her stories about the lake and how they fell in love. Although finding love on Rudyard Lake was the last thing I wanted in my life right now. I couldn't even entertain the idea of falling in love when my life was in such turmoil. I didn't even know my own purpose anymore. When my mom died, my capacity to love died with her.

"You will love the scenery around the lake, and it would be a perfect opportunity to paint. Now I know this may be a crazy idea, and we will respect your decision, whatever it may be, but know that the offer will stand. Your uncle and I are even planning to come out for a few weeks." She dropped her hands into her lap to let me know she was done.

I thought for a long time about her proposition. I wasn't one to accept change readily, or to change a course of action that I was on; I could thank my mom for that. But all of that was gone now, and I had to find my own way through life.

I hadn't been doing a very good job of it lately, either. Fights with Aunt Cathy for no reason, dismissal of all of my friends; I had basically become a miserable recluse. I buried my purpose in life right along with my mom in Garden of Faith Cemetery.

"I would like to think about it, but…" I stopped and grabbed Aunt Cathy's face with my eyes. "Thank you for the offer, really. I know you and Uncle Bern care for me deeply, and I love you both more than I could ever say." A new tear dropped out of my eyes, and I wrapped her in a hug.

My eyes scanned the room, this perfect little cottage in the middle of England. I wiped my eyes, knowing that the wave was reaching the shore and would stretch out and retreat any moment. I felt depleted, helpless, and entangled in emotion. As if retreating from a fog-covered forest, I emerged from the couch, wiped my eyes, and tried to focus on the surroundings and make sense of my new life, which I had been resisting for a long time.

Catching my reflection in the tiny mirror that hung on the wall at the bottom of the steps, I noticed that my hair had fallen around my face. The bun sat haphazardly on top of my head, and I yanked it free, letting my brown waves cross my shoulders. Jack was right, my eyes and my hair were the exact same shade of brown. I looked at my face, noticing many similarities to my mom. I had her eyes, lined by thick lashes, and her mouth, with a slightly thinner upper lip and fuller lower lip. My nose must be my father's. My mom's nose was always small and straight, whereas mine turned up slightly at the end. Mom always called it a button nose. I turned away from the mirror, wanting to know more about my father for the first time in my life. I had never asked much, my mom never really wanting to talk about him. I knew that now was not the time to start thinking about him, but one day I knew I would want to ask Aunt Cathy what she knew about him. I shook my head to rid myself of those thoughts and concentrate on what I had to do today.

I spent the rest of the day listening to music and calmly setting up my painting area in the living room. The background of a picture looking out over the lake from right inside the living room window was started. I lost myself in the process of painting, the mixing of colors, urging a ripple on the water from the tips of the paintbrush. I find a calm focus whenever I paint, and all the emotions left inside seep out onto the canvas.

By the time the sun went down, I settled on the couch with an iced tea and my laptop. Aunt Cathy would want an email letting her know how things were. I promised a few emails a week, and we would Skype on Sunday. Of course this didn't stop Aunt Cathy from texting me every day. Why had I taught her how to do that? A wordy email was scrambled off describing my day and trip to the Hollings Market. When I closed the lid on the laptop, I was caught by an image of Jack in my head. I chuckled to myself, and without even thinking, whipped out my phone and sent off a text to him.

Thanks for your help today. Ava

Shaking my head for doing something so uncharacteristically impulsive, I cleaned up and decided to spend the remaining hours in bed reading, my indulgence that was second to painting. Getting lost in a good book shuts off my mind to the crazy thoughts that sometimes play out when I have too much time on my hands.

I had trouble concentrating on the words as my brain decided it wasn't going to allow me to get lost. I decided to call it a night. I hated when my thoughts wouldn't shut off and let me concentrate. Too many emotions seemed to be running loose like a bunch of molecules in a pot of boiling water.

I placed the book on the nightstand, just as my cell phone blared. It was a text from Jack.

My pleasure Miss Banks.

I noticed the time stamp- 11:17. This was the second time I had seen it in one day. I shrugged my shoulders and settled down, wondering if I would visit with Katherine tonight. A part of me hoped I wouldn't and a long dreamless sleep would come and erase all the emotions that I continued to wear like a thick, winter coat.

Chapter 2

The song of the birds was getting closer and closer as I stood in the trees, trying to find my way out. They formed a maze that I followed with ease, however annoyed that I had to maneuver around the giant masses that only served to make my journey harder. When I reached the tree line, I felt like bursting from them and wishing them good riddance.

I stopped short, recognizing the familiar scene before me. The little wooden house and the barn to its left with the chicken coop on the periphery welcomed me back. I was standing on the dirt path that wove from the house out over the hill to the east. The scene before me itched at the back of my brain as if I were trying to remember something about it. I could smell the smoke billowing from the chimney, beckoning me inside to the warmth of the cozy house. The smell of the smoke lingered, like it was trying to find an itch to scratch.

Shaking my head, trying to clear my mind, I began to walk down the dusty lane. The sun was fading behind the barn which lay long shadows across the tiny flower garden that sat just in front of the house. I could barely make out a small figure bent over the flowers, and the sweetest song whirled around my ears. It was Becca, and she was singing that sweet tune I had heard her singing in the chicken coop.

Sensing that she wouldn't be able to see me, I was a little braver this time and walked right up behind her. I was strangely compelled to reach my hand out and stroke her long blond curls, feeling a peculiar love for this little girl. It was as if she belonged to me.

Just as I approached she stopped singing and slowly turned her head in my direction. I caught my breath and stooped down to her level. Could she see me? We were almost eye to eye and it was as if she was looking right into my wide brown eyes. She looked so sweet and innocent that I wanted to scoop her up in my arms. She smiled right at me, but at the same time she seemed to look right through me. Even so, I felt as if we were connected, and it was the most amazing feeling I have ever had. My heart swelled with love and amazement.

Very slowly she raised her hand, her eyes never leaving mine. I raised my hand to meet hers, but it was as if I was touching a cloud. There was an energy, very faint but present, in my fingers. Her brow wrinkled a bit like she was worried or maybe wondering just what was happening. With our hands suspended in midair touching but not touching, Becca resumed her song.

Birds in the branches

Sing songs from above.

High in the heavens

Sing a song of love.

"*Becca, time to come in and help with supper chores,*" *someone called from inside the house. Becca dropped her hand and giggled to herself as she swooped up her skirts and ran for the house. She paused at the door and glanced back in my direction before she ran through the doorway, almost as if she was motioning me in.*

I followed her toward the house as if mesmerized. The door hung open, and I resisted the urge to close it behind me as I stepped though the threshold. Finding a spot in the corner of the small space, I wanted to watch the happy scene before me.

The room was small but neat. A wooden table was set in the center with five chairs crammed in around it. A rocking chair and another wooden arm chair were set off to the other side. To the left was another tiny room. I could see the fire flickering below the black kettle that was spewing a cloud into the air. I caught the scent almost immediately and breathed in the most delicious aroma.

From around the corner a woman emerged carrying a basket full of something green. She set the basket on the table. The tall woman looked lost in her long skirt, petticoats, boots and apron. She looked as if the bulk of clothes could swallow her up.

Her light brown hair was wound round and round on top of her head. A worn and weary look on her face gave her the appearance that she was once more beautiful and happier than she appeared now.

"Here you go, sweetie, get these ready for the pot, please, and close the door; the wind is picking up out there." She leaned down and kissed the top of Becca's head and went back to the kitchen.

Gabriel and Katherine burst through the door as if they were racing inside. Gabe almost slammed into the table and grabbed the sides as he let out a chuckle.

"I win!" he proudly announced.

"Katherine, clean up please, and come give me a hand. Gabriel, your father will be expecting you in the barn to help unhitch the team." Their mother's voice radiated from the kitchen, not giving them even a chance to catch their breath.

Gabe rolled his eyes and bounded back out the door, slamming the door on his exit. Katherine went into the kitchen and was lost from my view. I felt comfortable and almost at home in this little house, and I wanted to hum along with Becca.

There was a knock on the door, and Becca went to open it up. Her face lit up, and she squealed with delight at whoever stood just beyond the threshold.

"Katherine, Johnny is here," she called as she leapt into his arms, giggling into his shoulder as he hoisted her up and carried her in, planting her back on her seat.

This boy was tall and thin, dressed in brown overalls with a blue shirt and a brown hat poised on his head. He was stunning, with wide green eyes that laughed as he patted Becca's head and took the seat next to her. I couldn't take my eyes off of him. His dirty blond hair hung below his hat, almost shading his eyes. As soon as I saw him, I knew him; it was the strangest feeling, like I knew him through Katherine's eyes. The way you feel when you see a sunset over the ocean for the first time.

As if I drew her out of the kitchen, Katherine came from around the corner, wiping her hands on her apron, a faint blush forming on her cheeks.

"Hello, John, what brings you here?" She looked down at the floor, and even with this brief exchange, I could see the love in both of their eyes, feel it in my heart.

"Mama made some fresh nut bread and asked me to bring some over. Of course, I never turn down an offer to visit my

favorite gals." He patted Becca's head sending her into a fit of giggles again.

"Thank you, John, please send our thanks to your ma. How is she holding up?"

"Oh, as well as can be expected. I am working overtime to get the crops ready in time for harvest, but so far it is all working out for us. Pa's brother is expected to arrive any day to finish up the harvest for us."

"Good to hear."

Katherine sat down across from him and their eyes locked. A smile formed on her lips as the blush spread over her face. She reached across the table to take the bread and let the back of her hand linger at the side of his hand. The current that ran through Katherine's arm to her heart did the same to me, and I put my arms around my waist to steady myself.

Ma walked into the room forcing Katherine to pull her hand away and the blush to rise higher on her cheeks.

"Johnny Cooper, it is sure nice to see you. Thank your ma for the bread; that was awfully nice of her. Won't you tell her that I was planning to call on her this week?"

"I sure will, Ma'am."

"Katherine, your chores are not done in the kitchen, so just visit a few minutes longer. You know your father will be ready for his supper when he walks in that door."

I thought I saw Katherine shutter a little bit before her reply.

"OK Mama. Can I walk John out to the lane, please?"

"OK dear, but hurry up. Rebecca, you can walk with them." Katherine glowered at her mom's back as she returned to the kitchen.

The three rose and headed out the door with me quick on their heels. They walked in silence to the lane, making it as far as the massive oak tree, hoping it would shade them from the house. When they stopped, John scooped Becca up into his arms.

Looking at Katherine, he spoke to Becca, "Hey Bug, why don't you run over to that gorgeous flower garden of yours and pick me a few of the best looking flowers for me to take home to my mama?" He set her down on the ground, and her feet were already moving toward the garden, singing her song about the birds.

John moved a bit closer to Katherine and grabbed for her hands. They stood, hands locked together, staring into each other's eyes for a long time. Slowly, but with a sense of urgency, he lifted her hands to his mouth and pressed his lips to them, never taking his eyes off of hers. He inhaled her scent as his lips lingered on her hand. Knowing that he didn't have long before Becca would return, he squeezed her hands.

"I've missed you, Kat." She didn't reply; the look in their eyes said it all.

Becca was running back toward them now, so they had to drop their hands, but the emotion between them was so palpable. I realized a tear was forming in my eyes just watching this beautiful exchange.

"Thanks Bug, these are perfect." He took his tall frame down to her level and winked at her, which was more than she could contain. Becca squealed and covered her face in her hands.

John, having returned to full height, stole a wink in Katherine's direction before heading up the lane. Both Becca and Katherine stared after him as long as they could.

"Come on, Katherine, I can see Pa coming over the hill, we better get moving." Becca grabbed at Katherine's skirt, her face, which was joyous a moment ago, carried an edge of worry now.

I tried to follow them, not wanting this to end, but I was glued in place. I couldn't move my legs, as if my brain and my body were in communication failure. The more I tried to move, the harder it became, and my mind began to fade, as if it were filling up quickly with water, drowning out pieces at a time.

I woke up feeling drained and annoyed. As I snuggled farther down under the blankets, I just wanted to escape from the lingering feelings of love and family that kept invading my sleep. Witnessing the love between Katherine and John wasn't enough, I had to feel it in my heart as well, and it felt like an unwelcomed intruder.

I had a hard time coming back to my reality. These dreams were so real, as if I had been transported back in time to a real place and real events while I slept. I was used to dreams that didn't make much sense, ones that jumped around and struggled to linger when I woke up. Waking up feeling as if I had lived another life while I slept was very unsettling and put me in a bad mood.

Starting out the day in a mood was not good for the overall emotional state. It made me think of my mom and the loss of my life as I knew it. I couldn't understand why I would be dreaming about this family. It was like the love between Katherine and John was being rubbed in my face.

I groped my way out of bed and dressed in my faded and well- worn sweat shorts and t-shirt and threw my robe on over top to take off the morning chill. Memories of my mom and my childhood started spilling out into my mind; they clouded my reality, and I had to force myself to look beyond them. There were just some memories I wasn't able to face yet.

I had planned on cleaning the cottage today and wanted to check in with Aunt Cathy about their pending visit. If all went well, they would be here in four weeks and hoped to stay for three if Uncle Bern's job could be without him that long. I would then leave with them. It seemed like it was so far away, but I also felt like I never wanted it to come for some odd reason.

As I stepped out on the patio, I could just make out a shape far out on the lake, standing on top of the wooden platform that floated about 100 yards out. I hadn't given this square piece of wood a second thought since I had arrived, but now I didn't have a choice. When it was built it had probably been a floating dock of sorts for swimming.

The shape took focus, and I realized it was Jack out there. What on earth was he doing? He spotted me, waved, and dove into the water. Before I knew it he was shaking himself off as he strode up the yard toward me.

"What are you doing?"

"I decided to fix this floating dock for you."

"For me?" Did it even belong to this house? I couldn't

contemplate this long as cold drops of water were raining down on me as Jack shook his head back and forth. His laughter followed.

"Geesh Jack, that was unnecessary."

"Chill, just having fun." Jack punched me in the arm as he took off toward the house.

"Got any coffee? I need a jolt before going hiking."

He strolled right into the house like he owned it, and I didn't have a choice but to follow him, my irritation rising. As I made us both coffee; I had to find out just what he was doing.

"So what gives? Why are you out there fixing that heap of wood? And who said anything about hiking today anyway?"

"Woke up about 5:30 and couldn't fall back to sleep. I was out on the canoe yesterday and noticed that old thing. It looked like it needed an overhaul and… um… I thought I could tackle it this morning."

"Well thanks. I will let Uncle Bern know. He will appreciate it." I looked at Jack while he drank his coffee and ate my last cinnamon bun which he snuck off the counter.

"So you said you are going hiking today?"

"WE are going hiking today," he corrected. "I thought I would take you deep into the woods on the other side of the lake.

Great trails through the trees, and at the top of one of the hills you get an amazing view of Leek. It's one of my favorite hikes."

"Um, no, thank you. I have things I need to do."

"Like what? Come on, it will be fun. You said it yourself yesterday, that you liked to hike. The weather is perfect, and I am not taking no for an answer."

"I really don't want to. I have plans, and I am not in the mood to hike."

"All the more reason to get out and enjoy the fresh air. Come on Ava, what do you have to do anyway? Can't be more important that spending the day with me." He puffed up his chest and flashed me his smile.

"You really aren't going to let me say no are you?"

"Nope, now go shower and get ready. Oh, and I need to hop in the shower after you? If you don't mind. Rinse off the lake water and all." He flashed me that smile again that sent chills down my back.

"Aren't we a bit presumptuous Mr. Hollings?" I asked, the irritation slowly creeping up my neck, replacing the chills.

I stomped upstairs mildly annoyed that Jack wanted to take a shower here. What bothered me so much about it? I couldn't really put my finger on why this bothered me; it was lost in the inner workings of my mind.

I spent longer on my hair than I normally do, taking out my aggravation. Who did he think he was marching in here like that? When my brown, wavy hair was brushed straight and pulled back in a pony tail, I looked in the mirror and forced a smile. "At least I will be spending the day outside with amazing scenery," I said to my reflection, trying to find something positive, which had been so difficult for me lately. Really I was just drained and tired and wished that Jack Hollings would just leave me alone, yet I couldn't explain the smile that had crept up on my face in the reflection.

Jack was sitting on a tree stump out in the yard, staring out over the lake. I stopped and watched him from the patio; he hadn't heard my approach. He was more muscular than I had originally thought; his thighs hugged the stump perfectly. His arms rested on them naturally as his biceps shown from the bottom of his shirt sleeves. There were so many different feelings I was experiencing, almost as if Jack stirred up some distant emotions. It was a strange feeling, as if a deep part of me was beginning to churn, as if my thoughts were no longer mine. I couldn't make sense of it.

"Hey, not stinky anymore?"

I picked up a stick and threw it at him. "Whatever, Jack. Well, get in there, if you must take a shower."

"I'm on it, sir!" Jack picked up a small duffle bag and ran to the house, dumping a basket of leaves on my head as he passed. UGHHH! I ran after him into the house, but he was already up the stairs as I stood in the foyer with leaves falling down all over the floor.

"Ughhhh! You are infuriating!" I said to the waft of lake air left in his wake.

It didn't take me long to get the leaves up off the floor and myself cleaned up, and Jack was back down the stairs in a pair of jeans, wet hair and no shirt. I paused for a minute glimpsing at his muscular chest. Years of rowing, fishing, and life on the lake had left his abs taught. I had to look away once again to hide the blush and unexplained smile.

"Put a shirt on, will ya?"

Jack watched me blush as he pulled his navy t-shirt over his chest, amusement written all over his face. Our eyes met as his emerged from the top of the shirt. I held his gaze longer than I normally would have, and all the irritation I had felt earlier seemed to melt away. I smiled and turned to retrieve my shoes from behind the couch.

Because I refused to canoe or even entertain the thought of any other mode of transportation across the lake, we had to follow the winding paths 3 miles around the lake. By the time we reached the other side, the sun was high in the sky. I was so lost in the stunning scenery that I didn't pay too much attention to Jack's babbling. Instead I was listening to the song of the birds high above us, the gentle babble of the lake as it lightly rolled over the rocky, sandy shoreline. One of the red birds was calling to another, and it sounded like he was singing, "Birdy birdy birdy." The response came from farther down the lake, "Birdy birdy birdy." I smiled at their exchange.

The trees and shrubbery took on a life of their own as I passed by, gliding my fingers over anything in reach. They swayed with me as I walked by and even seemed to part the way for me. I tried to keep one small part of my brain wrapped around Jack's amusing voice so that I wasn't caught in my musing over nature. I loved listening to his accent, sometimes paying more attention to how he was saying certain words instead of what he was actually saying.

"So the birds make these tracks along the sand where we are headed. The different bird tracks and the pictures they create in the sand are brilliant." Jack's reference to nature pulled me out of my trance. "It's like this cool bird meeting place, where they gather and peck around in the sand together." Jack's giggle reverberated off the hillside.

"I would like to see that." I told him, mentally rolling my eyes at his boyishness.

We wound our way around trees and branches as the path started to incline. The path doubled back on itself several times as it lazily meandered up the hill. Jack and I went slowly, sometimes silent and concentrating on our steps and each breath, grabbing low hung branches for support along the way. Other times Jack prattled on about this or that, and all I could hear was his thick accent punctuating certain words. From his prattle, I learned that he had lived here for 7 years, since he was 10. His parents sold their London flat and bought the cottage and market on the lake, and they had never been happier. Jack was about to finish his last year of school and wasn't sure about going to University in the fall or just staying on the lake and expanding his own lake tour and nature sightings business.

The air around us became damp and heavy in my lungs. Jack helped me up one particularly steep, slippery area of dirt and rock. He extended his hand to me just as I reached for it, no words spoken, as if we could read each other's minds and had done this a million times before. I shook my head at the nonsense invading my thoughts, set my feet right on the path, and continued on without looking at him.

We decided to stop for lunch at the top of a steep slope with gorgeous views of the lake and surrounding towns. Fluffy clouds dotted the sky and the heat of the day was settling all around us as Jack found a small clearing and set down his pack. Leave it to him to come prepared, I hadn't even thought about food and only brought my water bottle after Jack asked me where mine was as we started out the door. I was beginning to appreciate Jack's presumptuousness as my stomach rumbled.

I couldn't believe what materialized from the pack. A small square cloth was the first to arrive, and he laid it out with care. Next came the cheeses and breads, which had Hollings Market written all over them. Salami and fruit followed, and Jack looked at me with pride all over his face.

"Elise sure packed us a great lunch," I chided.

"Hey now, this was all me; not my first day on the job!" Jack scooped up some cheese and his bread and began to eat. "What, didn't think I know how to feed myself."

"Whatever. Give me some of that kiwi; that looks amazing."

We ate in silence for awhile, looking out over the lake. I could make out a few boats from the marina.

"Those yellow ones are training boats. We use them to teach children how to sail."

I looked closely at the one that was closest to us. I could just make out the words on the side: Rudyard Sailing School, followed by a number- 1117. I crinkled my nose wondering why that number seemed to be following me.

Farther in the distance I could make out the angled building tops of a sleepy, little town. The architecture rolled along with the distant hills as if it were a part of the ancient landscape. Wispy clouds dotted the skyline. I could also make out birds flying in the distance and was musing about how I would paint them into a picture.

Jack was unusually quiet, and I should have known what was coming next.

"So you are going to University in the fall, in the states? What's your plan?"

Jack leaned back on his elbows and appraised me carefully.

I sat for a long time, trying to decide what to tell him. I just wasn't sure I was ready to pour my life out to him.

"I was accepted into the Art History program at Stanford," I squeaked out between bites. Please just leave it at that, Jack!

"California, that's bloody brilliant! You must be so excited!!! Your parents must be so proud."

And there it was; I stared out over the lake, willing the tears to stay away. They pricked at the back of my throat. It was amazing to me how easily they could be summoned, as if they were just sitting there waiting for their chance to spring free. It was useless; the tears always won.

"Hey, hey now, what's wrong? I'm sorry, I didn't mean to make you cry." He gave me a quick jab at my arm which turned into more of a rub.

And just like that I poured out my story as if someone else was controlling my words and I had retreated somewhere deep inside to hide.

"I never knew my father; he was never a part of my life. It was just me and my mom. She worked hard as a school nurse and sometimes worked two jobs to make ends meet. On the day I got my acceptance letter, my mom died in a car crash on her way home from work." I stared down at my feet, not allowing myself to meet Jack's eyes.

"She never knew I had gotten into Stanford." I turned away from Jack so he wouldn't see the pain on my face. We sat in silence for awhile, looking out over the lake. Neither one of us knew what to say; I was grateful for the silence.

After a few minutes he said, "Thank you for sharing that."

I nodded and wiped my face with the napkins he brought. We silently cleaned up the mess, and when everything was packed in his backpack he put out a hand to help me up. Before I could get all the way up, Jack's arms were around me. His arms around me felt comforting and welcomed.

"Just because I said I had gotten into Stanford doesn't mean I am going to go." I mumbled into his shoulder. He squeezed me a little bit tighter, and even though he didn't say anything, I could feel the smile. When I broke free first, my eyes caught his and I stared into the deep green. They held such warmth and calm and felt so familiar that I struggled to pull away from them. I thought he was going to lean in to kiss me, and I hesitated, not sure if I wanted him to or not. My inner struggle was broken by his boyish giggle as he let go of my arms and stooped to pick up his pack.

Heading down the slope toward the beach and path, Jack was his usual jovial self, whistling a familiar tune and occasionally throwing leaves back at me. I let these pass because I felt like being quiet for awhile. His tune filled my mind, yet I just couldn't place it, even though I knew I had heard it before.

I was mad at myself for sharing so much with Jack; I wasn't used to being so vulnerable. There was just something about Jack that made me feel safe, and I wasn't sure I liked it…yet. I just hoped he wouldn't ask any other questions about my past; I wasn't ready to share anything else with him.

At the beach, Jack pointed out the bird tracks that dotted the beach. He knew all of the wildlife around the lake, and I loved hearing his excitement over each new track. The beautiful collection of tracks laid out a glorious nature painting. I made a mental note to bring my easel over to paint this little scene. He pointed to something in the distance, across the lake near the end.

"See the cottage between the two large trees? That is the market."

I looked up at him, questioning with my eyes, and took my camera out of my pocket. I zoomed in on the cottage and snapped a few pictures.

We spent the afternoon searching out creatures, birds, and other wildlife along the lake as we wound our way back toward my house. We got back about 5:00, and I was starving. I decided to make some spaghetti for us. After all, he did spend the day taking me around the lake; the least I could do was make him something to eat. I wasn't sure if I wanted him to leave just yet but wasn't really sure why.

While I made dinner, he swept off the patio and fixed the squeaking patio door. When everything was ready, I had to hunt him down. He was floating in the water.

"What on earth are you doing? Dinner is ready and getting cold! I yelled out to him as I approached the dock.

"Chill, missy?, I was just washing off the day. A nightly dip in the lake is a ritual of mine." This made me shutter; I would have to run right for the shower if I had done that. He didn't even have a towel. Wait! I looked a bit closer and saw that he wasn't wearing anything.

"Jack, where are your clothes? What on earth are you doing?" It never dawned on me that he would pull himself up on the dock and head right for me. Before I could register just what he was doing, he was almost standing right in front of me.

"Well, aren't you the exhibitionist? I'll go get you a towel." Rolling my eyes, I hurried off to the house and draped a towel on the patio chair. He would have to find it for himself. I had seen enough of Jack Hollings for one day.

Halfway through my salad, he walked in, dried off and thankfully fully clothed. I guess both of us exposed a little more than we had anticipated today. Although something told me that Jack didn't view his nakedness the same way I viewed sharing my life story.

"Sorry if I embarrassed you out there," he said as he took his seat. "Hey! This looks great, thanks! I don't care what they say about you, you're alright Ms. Banks."

"Thank you, it's not anything great. I would love to spend the day in the kitchen with your mom; I'm sure she could teach me a few things. I really like your parents, you know. I can tell they are good people. Not sure how they had an arrogant, immature, exhibitionist for a son though."

"Oh, she CAN dish it out! Good one, Banks! I knew you had it in you." His accent made me stifle a giggle.

Before I knew it I had reached out to punch him in the arm. There was something about Jack that reached deep inside and brought out parts of me that I didn't even know existed.

"So, do you have a girlfriend?" Now where did that come from? It was if I no longer had control of my thoughts.

"I did," was all he said, and he shrugged his shoulders and shoveled some more spaghetti into his mouth, closing the subject.

I let it go at that. I wasn't entirely sure why I had even asked, and he certainly didn't seem to want to offer more. I could appreciate that. He looked at me and shrugged his shoulders again, officially closing the subject.

Jack helped me clean up and then began to gather his things. The light was fading, and I didn't like the idea of him walking home alone.

"Thanks for today, I really enjoyed seeing more of the lake and especially learning about all of the bird tracks." I moved to the other side of the kitchen, wanting to put some distance between us.

"I have campers again tomorrow morning, and then I promised Dad I would help him in the shop. Maybe I will see you later in the week?" He was just at the door when he added, "Maybe this weekend we could plan another hike or get your sea legs wet on the canoe?"

"Jack, I am not getting on that canoe, or anywhere near that water. Have a good time, and tell Elise and James I said "Hi." I am sure I will be down to the market this weekend to restock after you ate all my spaghetti and salad." I returned this with a big smile which felt fake on my face but just right in my heart.

"OK, I will see you this weekend then." And he was gone. I watched him bound back up the hill. The wind carried a familiar sound through the window, and Jack was humming that familiar tune again. It was gone with him down the lane before I could figure out what it was.

I went to sleep thinking about Jack. I had the feeling that I wasn't going to be able to get rid of him this summer, and I wasn't sure how I felt about that. My mind also seemed to do funny things around him, and I certainly didn't like it. It was as if I had little control of what I was thinking or my actions, something that I was completely unfamiliar with and ill-prepared to deal with. Something itched at the back of my brain as I fell asleep, some distant thought that I couldn't quite grasp. Sleep erased it as quickly as it had come.

Chapter 3

The field stretched out before me in all directions. Tall, flowing grains dotted the landscape only disturbed by two tall figures on the horizon. I seemed to cover the distance in one quick stride, not at all disturbing the delicate beauty of the swaying wheat all around me. I found myself standing close enough to the two men that I could reach out and pluck their straw hats right off their heads.

"If we work hard enough, we can get them all in before the first frost."

"I don't know about that, Albert. I wish Johnny were old enough to help us."

"Well, he isn't yet, so it's just me and you. If we work sun up to sun down we can do it, I know we can."

I realized that my hand was covering my mouth, holding back the gasp that wanted to escape. Watching Katherine and John's fathers seemed so wrong, like it didn't belong to the place that I was starting to get to know. Katherine's pa looked so young and I could see little Becca's eyes laughing as he slapped John's pa on the back and picked up the scythe. Pa began whistling the same tune that I had heard Becca singing as he and

John's pa quickly and deftly harvested their precious grain. The two men worked side by side as if they were one.

I scanned the surroundings and could just barely make out the top of the tiny house I had come to know far off to the east. In the opposite direction I could see faint smoke rising from the tops of a chimney that could only be coming out of John's home. The two men seemed to be working at almost the halfway point between the two houses, but there was no obvious division of property line. Something, I am not sure what exactly, told me that these two men shared their crops, their work, and their friendship. It made me smile, but deep down something was telling me it just wasn't right.

The two men faded into the wheat as if swallowed up by the rustling crops, the wheat echoing the familiar tune that Pa was singing.

I woke with a start, sweating as if I were in the fields working right alongside the two men, the gleam of the sun still beating on my brow. I glanced at the clock: 11:17pm. It was almost as if this strange number on the clock had startled me awake. I rolled my eyes, trying not to give it too much thought, plumped up my pillow, and went right back to sleep.

The cold, hard stone could be felt right through my petticoat and skirt. I was perched on a rock in the middle of a long lane. Seated on two rocks up ahead were Katherine and

John. Their hands were entwined in his lap; their heads almost close enough to be touching. I scurried up ahead to join them.

"I don't understand it, John. Pa is just so different now, like he is a completely different person."

"My pa would know what to say if he were here. They were almost the same person, those two." John hung his head.

"No one can understand it. The Pa I used to know is just gone."

Katherine put her head on John's shoulder as he picked up her hands to kiss them.

"It's going to be alright. We will figure it out. Your Pa is a good man, we knew that once. He is still in there. We just have to figure out a way to find him again."

"It seems pointless, John, he is never going to approve of us. He has made that very clear. I just don't understand why. You would think he would be happy for our two families to finally be tied together."

"We always were anyway, until…"

"I know. I'm sorry." Uncharacteristically, Katherine turned her head up to kiss John. I could feel the kiss in my heart.

"Maybe one day it will change. Until then we will just have to be careful. I won't be 16 forever."

"I don't know how Ma and I can survive here on our own."

"Don't talk like that John. I can't bear to think about you going anywhere."

"It's definitely a possibility, Kat. I can't continue with school and tend to the crops myself. Uncle Gale's help will only last so long."

"Can we not talk about that right now? I have to get back to the house, and I hate spending what little time we have together talking like this."

"I'm sorry, you are right." John helped Katherine to her feet. "I want to show you something."

I followed them over the hill, and the three of us stopped at the top. John was pointing in the distance at a small lake and clearing that seemed to come out of nowhere, it didn't seem to belong on this horizon.

"That's it. The piece of land I was telling you about. That is where I want to build our home."

Katherine leaned her head on his shoulder. My heart pounded in my chest; I felt every emotion Katherine now had, happiness, eagerness, hopefulness, but also fear laying heavily over them all.

I woke up, my heart still pounding as Katherine's hope and fear mingled. I had trouble holding onto these dreams, and they quickly retreated into the recesses of my mind to mix with the other dreams that had been taking shape over the past few weeks.

It was hard to hold on to the details as they slipped away. Remembering them was like trying to grab a wisp of smoke. You know it is there, you can still smell it, but your fingers just can't take hold. A part of me didn't want to remember, yet I couldn't seem to forget. The lingering images of them stayed in the periphery of my brain. I would catch glimpses of them throughout the day, as if my mind was trying to hold onto them and didn't want me to forget.

I may have been painting a picture, or making the bed, pouring a cup of coffee, or talking to Aunt Cathy on the phone, and the image of Katherine would jump into my thoughts. Sometimes I could smell Pa's pipe or feel the gentle prairie breeze through my hair, even as the stagnant English summer air hung still around me.

I couldn't make sense of how real these dreams seemed. It both excited and scared me. I had never experienced any dream so real, almost as if a story were being played out in my head as I slept and I was an active player. Not wanting to give it too much thought for fear that I might be actually losing my mind, I tried to let go of my thoughts of them but found that almost impossible to do.

The need to explore and keep myself busy forced me outside, ready to find out more about this curious little lake and surrounding town. To the south of the lake sat a quaint little train station. The train whistle that I heard throughout the day beckoned me to find it. It was a nice walk from the cottage, and I would often take my coffee down there and watch the men get the small steam engine train ready for daily tourist rides around the lake.

The meandering track winds through the thick trees on the west side of the lake. I made it a point to ride the train at least once a week, always by myself, to grab a chance to get away from reality to sit by myself and think. The lake peeks in through the trees every now and again as if it's checking to make sure you are still there.

Sometimes I sat with random strangers that had also come to enjoy the ride: the parents who brought their children out for a train ride, the old couple enjoying a moment of peace and clarity, the lone passenger that rode the train to forget or to remember. We were all there for our own reasons, and I found it to be a very calming place, despite the sweet, high-pitched blast of the whistle that punctuated every other thought. When the train pulled out for its slow journey forward, things just seemed to melt away. For a few minutes, my mom wasn't dead, I was not alone in a strange country, and my heart just didn't ache as much. I probably would have ridden that train everyday if I had the money to be so frivolous. The men that ran the little station started to know me by name and always made sure that I had the perfect seat in the front of the train.

Two heavily bearded brothers, with thick British accents, ran the train station. They were quite a pair, and I loved to listen to them banter back and forth as they shoveled the coal into the tiny steam engine. From what little I had gathered, they had been running this railway for many, many years together. Everyone called them Edwards, both of them, which was really funny. They even called each other Edwards.

"Hey Edwards, look who it is, Miss Ava, back for another ride."

"Put her up front, Edwards."

"Good Morning." I usually kept my head down, not wanting the attention. I preferred watching them from afar, yet I didn't want to offend them, so I made sure to always greet them and thank them for the ride when I left. I think they knew that I wanted and needed the quiet time, and this made me like them all the more.

For hours after I left the station, I could hear the faint distant blare of the whistle. With each blast I could feel the peace and calm knocking to be let in. Sometimes I would let it overtake me, just for a few seconds, in the midst of whatever I was doing. I would stop and remember those feelings. But they were hard to hold, just like the evanescence of my dreams. The train was a constant reminder that life can be peaceful again, if I give it a chance, little by little. I was trying.

I was also trying with Jack Hollings. Telling him about my mom's death and how hard it had been for me was really difficult but at the same time cleansing. He didn't ask too many questions, he just let me share what I wanted to. He seemed to understand exactly how I was feeling without me even explaining it to him. He had never lost anyone close to him, but his ability to grasp my grief was astonishing to me.

He wasn't going to allow me to get too lonely out here as he often just showed up out of the blue or found some way to bother me. I tried not to think of him as a bother, but I wasn't ready to admit to myself that I might even enjoy his company. As was typical, Jack just appeared whenever he felt like it.

"Ava Banks, get out here and help me. Where are you? Come on, I know you are in there." I heard him yelling from the lake.

I peered out the bedroom window. Jack was standing in his canoe, rocking back and forth, head back, yelling like a little kid. The window flew up a little too hard with my frustrated shove.

"Jack, stop all of that yelling. I will be down in a minute."

I stomped down the steps, taking my irritation out on each creaking board. I stopped at the bottom of the steps and took a deep breath, just as the train whistle sounded.

"Stop taking your emotions out on him, Ava." My calmer self muttered as I swung open the patio door.

Jack was out of the canoe, pulling it up on the sandy edge. He reached into the bottom of the canoe and emerged with four long pieces of wood. They looked familiar to me, and as he got closer I could see that they were four freshly shaped oars for the canoe. He plopped them down on the soft ground at my feet.

"You and I are going to finish these today." His huge smile both irritated me and made me giggle.

"What?"

"You're the painter, so let's paint."

"I paint pictures on canvas, um, not wood."

"Chill, we are just going to varnish them today. After that dries, we paint. You'll have to let me know what kind of paint to get."

"To paint what?"

"Anything you want. On the paddles. These are yours."

"Jack, I don't want a canoe paddle. What on earth would I do with it?"

"I don't know, you'll think of something."

Jack wasn't taking no for an answer, and I found myself varnishing oars all day. It was a detailed process of sanding, coating, drying, rinse, repeat.

"There is something about working with wood that is comforting."

"If you say so."

"Dad and I made them; it took us a few weeks, but we got it done."

"Wow! That's pretty cool." Jack Hollings still found ways to surprise me.

"It's a great hobby. Next time you are at the house, I will show you the other things we have made."

Today Jack made me smile. I wasn't going to fight it because varnishing these little pieces of wood made me forget about things for just awhile. I had trouble with the sanding part, either applying too much pressure or not enough. Jack was very patient teaching me, very much like James would be.

"When you are sanding, you have to make sure you use even strokes." Jack showed me on his oar, gliding the sandpaper over the wood effortlessly.

"I just can't seem to get the hang of this."

"You will. Try going in one long, sweeping motion from one end to the other." Jack put his hand on top of mine, sending a jolt straight up my arm. I watched the concentration on his face instead of watching what he was showing me. His hand on mine felt firm but soft at the same time. He was close enough to me that I could smell the muskiness of his skin. It wasn't cologne, but his natural smell, and it was as if he was born of the pine needles and moss that surrounded the lake. I leaned in a bit closer and breathed in his smell. He turned to me.

"Ava, are you paying attention?"

"Oh, yes, yes, just like that, I think I got it now." I pulled my hand away a little too fast as the blush crept up my cheeks. Jack giggled and tweaked my nose.

"You are cute." He went back to sanding his oar and looked up occasionally to smile at me. My heart felt like it was melting.

I struggled to concentrate but eventually got the hang of it and was able to successfully sand my oars. The varnishing was easy, effortless, although the smell of the varnish made me crinkle my nose and seemed to erase the wispy feelings Jack's smell had given to me.

When Jack left, the paddles drying across the stools in the kitchen, the demons crept back in. I knew they wouldn't stay away for long, but Jack was gone, the train whistle silent for the night, and my mind began to think again. When I was with Jack or on the train, I was happy and could put away the difficult emotions for awhile. Falling asleep with tears was nothing new to me this year, and even being 3000 miles away from my home didn't stop it from enveloping me every chance it could.

The wind in my ears reminded me of the train whistle, and I had a hard time separating the two. I was standing on a platform of some sort. It didn't fit in the sprawling fields that lay out before me. I didn't recognize anything familiar as I sat down on the freshly sanded wooden planks. The breeze sang in my head, and I tried to shake the sound of the train whistle that came along with it. I searched the horizon for something to grab onto, something I recognized. Far in the distance I could see a horse carrying a man across the slash of sky and field.

As the breeze let up, I could make the sound out more clearly; it was a train whistle. It was out of place and unfamiliar in this place that I had come to know. The wind seemed to bring it closer to me with every breath. I sat and waited for something to happen, but nothing did. No train came, no people, nothing but me and the wind and the far off blasts of the train whistle.

Listening closely, it was as if it was trying to tell me something, but I couldn't figure out what it was. Like the birds at home, it seemed to be trying to communicate with me. I listened closely to the staccato of the blasts. It was a low sound that stretched out across the plain as if it were grabbing at each cloud in the sky, each tree. The blasts were punctuated with high, shrill, rhythmic sounds that carried with it a message.

"Carry on, carry on, carry on," it seemed to shout at me. Those were the words I heard in my head with each blow of the whistle. I scanned the horizon, searching for the telltale smoke that would accompany the whistle but found nothing. The wind was the only thing that remained.

As if a light switch had been flicked, I was instantly transported to another clearing, one more familiar. Standing in the middle of a wheat field, two children romped through the tall grains in front of me. It was clear, without even being able to see them, that it was a much younger Katherine and John.

"Johnny!" Katherine called over the fields.

"You can't catch me, Kat."

"I see you Johnny Cooper, and here I come."

Katherine ran straight towards John who dodged around tall stalks trying to lose her. Their laughter sang through the fields and echoed in my ears. Shielding my eyes from the sun, I could make out two men at the top of the field. One of the men had his hand on the other's shoulder as they watched the two children traipsing through the wheat.

I tried to run after them, but just as I picked up my leg to move, the wheat surrounded me and I fell forward, grasping for the ground.

I woke with a jolt, as if the bed caught my fall. I wanted to hold onto the carefree feeling that the dream left in its wake, but as I got ready for the day, the wave of emotion replaced it so easily. Feeling the need to escape it, I took my coffee down to the train station.

The 10:45 train was just pulling out of the station. As the whistle blared, I was immediately transported back to the wooden platform in my dream. "Carry on, Carry on, Carry on." The whistle blew in my ears. "I'm trying." I whispered to myself as I sat on the little bench and watched the tiny train disappear into the trees.

While I waited for the train, my mom kept popping into my head. I missed her so much and just wanted her here with me, and the thought that that was never going to happen again paralyzed me. A single tear escaped as I remembered back to that day.

I opened up the mailbox and nervously stared down at the letter from Stanford. I didn't want to open it, knowing that whatever lay inside would change my life in different ways. I gingerly carried the letter into the kitchen and stared at it for a few more minutes before frantically ripping it open.

Dear Ava Banks,

We are pleased to announce your acceptance to Stanford University in the Art History Program.

I didn't have to read anymore as I launched the letter into the air, jumping up and down around the kitchen. I don't remember ever feeling so happy. Stanford was my first choice after Aunt Cathy and Uncle Bern emphatically announced that they would cover all expenses for my education provided that I could get a scholarship, which this letter had announced that I had. I never thought that it would happen, but sometimes good things happen to those who persevere.

I grabbed the phone, wanting to call my mom but realized it was a few minutes after five and she would be in the car for her ride home. I took the letter out to the porch to wait for her 15 minute ride home. My legs nervously jumping up and down, I couldn't contain my excitement. I wanted to call Aunt Cathy but knew I had to tell Mom first, share the news with her before anyone else.

Five fifteen came and went. At 5:30 I called her cell phone, and it just rang and went to voice mail. I called Aunt Cathy.

"Aunt Cathy, is Mom there?"

"No darling, I haven't heard from her yet today."

"She's not home from work yet, and she usually calls me if she is stopping on her way home."

"I'm sure she is fine, but I will walk over and wait with you."

By the time Aunt Cathy arrived, I was a nervous wreck. The adrenaline rush of my acceptance was replaced with anxiety over where my mom was. At 6:25 our home phone echoed through the house. Fear gripped the back of my throat, making it hard to answer; no one ever called our home phone.

The next few days I don't even remember: the announcement that Mom had died on the way to the hospital, the funeral arrangements, and the stream of people's faces seen through my tears as they offered condolences. It was several weeks before I even told anyone about my acceptance to Stanford.

The train whistle blared in my ears, bringing me out of my reverie. I was so lost in thought that I hadn't even processed that the train had returned and most of the passengers had already disembarked. I quickly wiped my eyes and shook the painful memory from my head.

"Hey Miss America, you riding today?" Edwards' voice boomed in my ear. I nodded my head in response.

"Well come on then, the 11:15 is just getting ready to load. Hey Edwards, brush off that seat for Miss America, I'm sending her up." He motioned towards his brother and, grabbing my coffee mug, I walked slowly to the front of the train.

"Here you go Miss, nice and fresh seat for your trip."

"Thank you, Edwards." I grabbed his hand as he helped me into the seat.

"Get a goin' Edwards, it's 11:17, time to move on out!" Edwards shouted back to his brother, and the number seemed to punch me in the face. I recoiled, wondering what it was about that number.

The train ride was peaceful, and as always my mind cleared and I was able to enjoy a few peaceful minutes, the painful memory left on the train station bench. As the train rocked back and forth, I could clearly see Becca in my mind and thought about the electric connection that I had with her in the dream. It was a very curious thing that I had not allowed myself to think about before. I am not sure why that particular thought popped into my head, but that is just how it worked when I rode the train.

It was almost as if Becca knew I was there or sensed me there, and when we tried to touch hands, I was overwhelmed by a feeling of love for her. This perplexed me more than anything, yet I just couldn't help but think about her and the smile it brought me. I carried that feeling for the rest of the trip and actually felt better when I got off the train, thanked Edwards and Edwards, and started the walk back to the cottage. I decided to take the tree-lined path around the lake and enjoy the peaceful solitude that matched my mood.

About halfway there, my mind once again lost in thought, I literally stumbled upon Jack. He was sitting right in the middle of the path, twigs and dried leaves all around him.

"What on earth are you doing?"

"Nothin', what are you doing?"

"Seriously Jack, why are you just sitting in the middle of the path?"

"It's quiet."

"and....?" I sat down next to him, laughing to myself.

"Well, you seem happy today. Where are you coming from?"

"Just walking around the lake this morning." I didn't want to share my train rides with him.

"You know what today is, don't you?"

"Thursday?" I looked at him, questioning.

"June 21st, summer solstice, and the double sunset."

"Double sunset, what on earth is that?"

"Every year, on the summer solstice, there is this spot where you can see the sun set twice."

"How does that happen?"

"You have to see it, experience it. So what do you say? Sunset tonight? Is it a date?" I think as soon as he said it, he wished he hadn't. I saw the reluctance in his face.

"I'd like to see that." I couldn't believe what I had just said. I had even shocked myself.

"YES!" Jack jumped up and down like a little kid. He stopped when he noticed the strange way I was looking at him.

"Whatever, Miss Banks, you are going to love it."

"OK, well I am going now. So, have fun becoming one with the trees. I guess I will walk down to the market around 8:00."

"Nope, you are coming to dinner, around 6:00. Earlier if you want to, I'll be working on my boat."

"Your boat?"

"Yup, haven't named her yet, but Dad and I started building her over a year ago. He's let go of the reigns and is letting me finish her. I hope to have her in the water by August."

"I'll be down at 6:00. You sure your parents are OK with me coming for dinner?"

"Whose idea do you think it was? *They* like you." He nudged my side as he plopped himself back down on the ground. He folded his arms behind his head and lay back among the leaves. "See ya, Banks."

I shook my head at him and went back to the cottage. Double Sunset? This, I had to see.

I spent the afternoon working on my paintings, but my thoughts kept wondering back to Jack, and that was the last place I wanted it to go. I didn't need to be thinking about Jack. He was my friend, and I was not going to make anything of the crazy way my heartfelt around him, like I couldn't get enough oxygen.

Elise made a wonderful roast for dinner with Yorkshire pudding arranged to look like two suns. Elise and James filled me in on that evening's event while we ate.

"There is a peak over the town of Leek. The sun sets behind one side of the peak and then reemerges on the other side, only to set again over the hill. There are only a few places you can see it: next to a church in the middle of Leek, which is always so crowded with onlookers, or out in the middle of Rudyard Lake."

I almost choked on my food and had to very carefully chew it while digesting what James had just said.

"Out in the middle of the lake?" My shaky eyes met Jack's; he just shrugged. "Were you going to tell me this?"

"Um, didn't think it would really matter. We will have our own canoe, Mum and Dad have theirs."

"Ha ha, very funny, Jack. I am not going out on the canoe, and you know that." I wanted to get up and run away, but my legs wouldn't let me move. I was so mad at Jack; had he not heard a word I had told him about the canoe and how I felt about going out on the water? The irritation rose from my toes until my face darkened.

"It's OK, darling, we can try to see it from the shore. I'm sure there is somewhere?" Elise looked at James quizzically.

"I don't think so. I tried once to see it from the Sandpiper beach, but it wasn't the right angle.

"The little bird beach." Jack looked at me sheepishly, referring to the beach we had visited on our hike. I looked down at my hands.

"I'm sorry, Jack. Elise, James, I just can't do it. I'll see what I can see from my cottage. It's OK."

The mood had certainly changed, and as dusk approached, I was very quiet, helping Elise clean up the kitchen.

"You know, dear, it is OK to be afraid. I am sure that Jack just really wanted you to see it, but we all understand. We could drive in to Leek to try to see it from the Church."

"No no, don't change your plans. I am sure it is lovelier from the lake. Thank you for understanding." I hugged her and wanted so badly to just escape. "I think I should go, let you all get ready to leave. Thank you for dinner, as usual."

Elise tucked a bag with some containers inside under my arm after I said my goodbyes to Jack and James. I took another look back at Jack as I walked through the door. He was sitting on the couch looking dejected and so sweet it made me giggle.

My elation didn't last long as I slowly walked home in the shadows of the trees. I made sure that I was safe inside until well after sunset, when I made my way out of the patio. The moonlight was splashed across the lake like paint splatter. I wanted to capture this exact picture in my head so that I could recreate it on canvas, but somehow I knew it would just be lost like so many other things in my life. I was feeling more lost than ever as I climbed into bed and, thankfully, a dreamless sleep.

Chapter 4

Friday was devoted to painting. I had already started painting a picture of the house and barn in my dream. This one was just for me, so I kept it in my room and would paint very early in the morning when the dreams would take the best shape in my mind. Sometimes I would wake up and immediately go to the canvas and add a particular detail to the painting that I remembered from the last dream. It helped me hold onto the small details and emotions that surrounded each dream. Wanting to paint them made the dreams easier to deal with, and slowly I began to look forward to them. Sometimes while I painted I would get lost in remembering one of my favorite dreams.

Gabriel sat on a tree stump whittling something with a small knife. His face was hard and full of emotion. I walked up next to him and wanted to brush his curls out of his eyes. I could see tears glistening in his eyes as he worked the knife harshly over the pliable wood. The shavings gathered at his feet which he absent-mindedly swiped back and forth through the dirt.

I was just as startled as he was when Becca bounded up on the other side of him.

"Whatcha doin', Gaby?"

"Don't call me that!"

"Well, whatcha doin'?"

"Nothing." Gabe moved himself around on the stump farther from Becca so his back was to her.

Becca walked around to face him again. "Can I do nothing with you?"

"Get out of here."

"Come on Gabe, play with me? Katherine is busy with Ma in the house and I'm bored."

"Get out of here, Rebecca!"

Becca reacted to her full name as if he had slapped her across the face. The tears started with a sting, and she turned and ran into the barn. I glared at Gabriel, even though my heart wanted to reach out to him, and followed Becca into the barn.

I found her stroking the nose of one of the horses, her voice soft yet shrill.

"Will you play with me, Lady? No one else will." The horse answered her with a shake of his head and a soft whimper.

I walked right up to Becca and softly stroked her hair; a faint electric shock traveled up my arm. I felt her back stiffen as if she could actually feel me. Her head tilted slightly to the side, and I whispered softly to her, "I will play with you."

Becca giggled quietly and turned toward the end of the barn. She looked around and then skipped toward the far doors yelling, "Try to find me." She disappeared into the farthest horse stall, daring me to follow her. I could hear her giggles as she settled into a small hay pile in the corner.

Softly I followed after her, pausing at the door, wondering what she was thinking. Before I could venture any farther, I heard her soft voice, "Come find me," followed by her high-pitched giggle.

I peeked into the stall, the pungent smell of hay and dung clinging to my nostrils. My eyes came to rest on the top of Becca's head poking through the hay pile. I walked over close enough to touch her. She shook her head, letting hay fall all around her.

"Ha Ha, you found me!" She bounded out of the hay, almost knocking me over as she ran out of the stall with me close on her heels.

"Come find me," Becca giggled as she ran straight for the wooden ladder and began to ascend toward the loft.

I didn't have a choice but to follow her. Just as I got halfway up the ladder, Katherine appeared in the doorway. I froze mid-step, always startled by the fact that they couldn't see me.

"Becca? Are you in here? It's time to come in. Ma needs your help with supper." I could hear Becca rustling around above me, trying to keep still and quiet.

"Come on, Becca, I can hear you. Come down here now." Katherine looked annoyed, hot and tired. I descended the stairs and walked over to her tentatively. I could see the exhaustion and worry in her eyes.

"Aw Katherine, you always ruin everything. I was playing hide and go find."

"It's hide and go seek, baby girl."

"Stop calling me baby girl! I am not a baby, and I will call it whatever I want." Becca stomped out the door.

Katherine stood where she was, staring through the barn walls ahead of her. Her thoughts were a million miles away, and I could see a single tear slide down her cheek as she heaved a sigh and turned toward the door. A single word escaped her lips as she pushed through the door into the sunlight. "John."

It was dreams like this that made me wake up in a vivid, almost too colorful state. Everything was clear and bright, and those were the days I liked to paint the most. I had given up trying to figure out why I was having these all too real story-like dreams and used them for motivation in my paintings.

In the living room, I was working on a scene of the lake for Elise and James, using the picture of the Market I had taken from the other side of the lake. I kept this covered so Jack wouldn't see it and spoil my surprise. I took extra care to paint every detail. I wanted to get it right and poured my heart and soul into it.

Luckily I had it covered when Jack showed up with no warning, as he so often did. I came to expect it at some point nearly every day.

This day, he came in from the lake. He was wet, and as I looked past him out the window, I saw his canoe bobbing on the water's edge.

"What's up?"

"Just painting. What's up with you?"

"Paddling around."

"Sounds fun." I rolled my eyes at him.

Jack plopped down on the couch and hung his leg over the side.

"Let me finish this one part, and I'll hop in with ya and we can paddle around the lake."

"WHAT?" Jack nearly fell off the couch. "Are you serious?"

The smile gave me away, and when he realized I was joking he lunged off the couch and pushed me off my stool. I faked hurt, and we both laughed about it. He watched me finish a small twig of a tree with rapt attention. I didn't want to tell him about it. Part of me didn't like sharing what I was doing; fortunately he didn't ask. While I finished and cleaned off my brushes and generally straightened things up, Jack was setting up the Scrabble board on the patio.

As I rolled my eyes at his presumptuousness, I was secretly glad to have something to do, and Jack was amusing me today for some reason. I think I had decided to just accept him for who he was and not let his childishness bother me.

My phone rang from somewhere deep in the house, and as I rose to run and grab it, my knee upturned the Scrabble board.

"Hey now, your boyfriend can wait."

"Jack, knock it off! I'll be right back."

I ran into the house to grab the phone, and Jack was muttering something to himself as he set the board back up.

"Hello?"

"Hi sweetie, how's life?"

"Aunt Cathy! It's great!! How are things back home?"

"Just fine, sweetie, Uncle Bern is busy as ever at work, but we are so excited for our trip! I want you to email me anything we can bring you! We were talking last night about taking you into London and the National Gallery."

"That's great, Aunt Cathy, thanks. I was hoping to get there during my stay. Everything here is great. Jack is keeping me busy, and I have three paintings started."

"Honey, that is fantastic. We are so proud of you."

"It's awfully early Aunt Cathy, what are you doing up this early?"

"Well, let's see, it's 6:17 and I have already been up for an hour. Snoring, you know. Your uncle has never been the silent type."

I mentally did the math, making it 11:17am here- hrumph. I shook it off, and my heart warmed thinking about my uncle who was anything but the silent type.

Aunt Cathy went on to tell me about running in to a friend of hers, Sylvia Manns, at the market over the weekend. Her son was also going to Stanford, and she wanted me to meet him before I left for school. I cringed and held my tongue, not letting on that anything had changed, but forcing me to remember that I would have to tell her sooner or later.

"Well, we still have time for that. For now, I am good, quite happy, really. I will call you this weekend, K?"

"Bye, darling, we love you."

"Love you, too! Kisses to Uncle Bern, when he wakes up."

When I hung up, I clung to Aunt Cathy's words and rested the phone against my cheek. I looked down at the screen just as the number of minutes we talked was fading away- 11:17.

"Ughhh, this is getting annoying." I put the phone back on the counter and went to rejoin Jack.

He was sitting on the patio with the Scrabble board in front of him, making random words across the board. His face looked peaceful; random happy thoughts brightened his eyes. I smiled at my new friend.

When I walked out on the patio I saw the words: "canoe" with the word "fun" descending to the n. Feigning to trip, I knocked the board, sending the letters sprawling again.

"That's what I think of your words."

"Ha ha, hilarious."

Jack leaned across the board to retrieve the letters just as I sat down on the concrete, and our heads banged. Rolling off the concrete onto the mossy ground, clutching our heads, we broke into laughter that echoed off the trees. With both of us sprawled out on the mossy lawn, I looked over at Jack and our eyes met. All I could hear was the lapping of the lake water on the rocky shore as our eyes spoke to each other momentarily. I am not sure who broke first, but that brief exchange sent a buzz through my body which I had never felt before, and it was certainly out of my control.

Five games later, with three wins under my belt, the rain started, and Jack and I were forced inside. He put the game back into the old hutch that Aunt Cathy had painted a warm, vanilla color and carefully stenciled ivy along its edges. It stood in the living room and held games, old magazines, and books along with other various articles of need. The whole cottage was an eclectic mix of antiques and old throw away pieces of furniture that Aunt Cathy had refurbished. It was a perfect blend of old and new and made me feel cozy. There was the ancient child's stool that should have splintered and been thrown away many years earlier, taking with it all the memories of little children's feet. Instead it stood proudly in the corner with a renewed spirit thanks to the white paint and stenciled on daffodils.

I was busying myself making us some lunch when Jack came in with something waving in front of him.

"Look what I found in that old hutch."

I grabbed what looked like a picture from him. It was two people standing out by the lake, arms wrapped around each other. I could tell that they were standing on the lawn right outside of the cottage, but the trees looked shorter, the woods thinner than they are now.

Words had been cut out of a magazine and placed precariously in the sky. The words read, *"Our dream, our life".* I stared more closely at the people and realized it was Aunt Cathy and Uncle Bern many years ago. Aunt Cathy looked exactly the same except much, much younger. She even had the same short hair cut in a bob around her face. It made me laugh thinking about her at my age.

I almost didn't recognize Uncle Bern. He was so thin and striking. I only knew it was him because of the dimple on the right side of his mouth when he smiled. Other than that I would have thought it was someone else, he looked so young.

My eye caught the words again, and it made me stop and wonder exactly what it meant.

"Wow, this is so cool. I can't wait to show it to them when they get here. What do you think it means?"

"I'm not sure. Probably nothing." Jack's face looked far away, lost in thought.

"Here, let me put it back in the hutch for when they get here."

"No, wait, I think I might want to try to paint this one."

"But you don't do people."

"I don't know. There is something about this picture makes me want to try. I love the words in the sky. The least I can do is frame it for them." I put the picture on the counter, but something was bothering me about the words. I tried not to give it too much thought, but my mind didn't want to let it go. Jack seemed just as lost in thought as I did.

Seeing that picture of Cathy and Bern made me think about my mom, and the emptiness began to creep through my body like a fever. Just as my mind was about to travel down a very slippery slope, the train whistle called me back to reality. At that very moment, I craved it, I wanted to take that peaceful ride around the lake, and it was like it was calling me. I looked at the clock; it was 3:00. There would be one more train before they closed for the day.

"So if I asked you to do something with me, would you do it without asking any questions?" It was the only way I could think to be able to take the ride and not have to kick Jack out for a strange reason that would just bring about his annoying questions.

"Sure will. What you got in mind?"

"I want to ride the Rudyard Steam." I didn't want to look at him. "I've already been on it a few times, but I really want to go ride today."

Jack hopped off the couch and clapped his hands together. "Let's go." He grabbed my hand, and we were out the door before I realized what had just happened. As we turned onto the lane, I dropped his hand, pretending to cough.

"So I have to also ask another favor."

"Sure thing, I am all about appeasing tonight."

"Can you sit in your own seat, behind me?"

"Um OK, why?"

"I said no questions."

"OK, whatever you say. Can I at least sit in the same train car?"

"Yes, goof. Come on, we are going to miss it."

We ran down to the station. Edwards sold us a ticket and ushered us on to the other Edwards with a wink. I rolled my eyes at him as Edwards motioned us up to the front car. I took my seat up front while Jack squeezed in the seat behind me.

As soon as I sat down, the weight seemed to lift, and I straightened my shoulders up a bit to take the wind. I could feel Jack shifting in the seat behind me. I looked over my shoulder and saw that he had moved farther down the seat so that he could see the side of my face. I glowered at him and turned forward just as the train lurched. Even though I could sense him staring at me, I let myself get lost in the motion of the train, the quiet sounds of the water rippling, and the gentle sway of the trees that hurried by us.

I felt the empty bliss, the escape, the nothingness that followed. My mind went still, and for the whole 25 minutes, I was able to forget. So much so that when we returned to the station, I think Jack was a bit freaked out.

"Stop looking at me like I'm a zombie! I just like to be quiet and by myself sometimes." I gently nudged his shoulder as we walked back down the length of the train.

"I like it; you seemed happy."

"I am trying."

Jack didn't respond, and I was glad. Instead, we walked back to the cottage quietly. I watched Jack from the corner of my eye, wondering how he always knew just what I needed.

"Wanna stop by the market on the way back to your cottage? I ate your last bun." Jack's childish grin made me laugh.

"Yes, and this time I am putting them under lock and key."

We bantered back and forth until we reached the market. Jack went right to the bakery to help his dad, and I gathered the few things I needed and took them up to the counter. James would bag them and bill me later and bring everything over to the house to store until I was ready to leave. It had become a routine now.

I found Elise reading a book in her chair. She looked so peaceful and content and it warmed my heart.

"Hello darling, come sit."

"What are you reading?"

"Oh, just a collection of poems that I have always loved. James gave them to me as a teenager when we met."

"How did you meet?"

"It is a sweet story. I was still in Comp and James had already started Uni. My parents brought me to the lake to swim and fish one summer day. James was with a few of his buddies fishing from a canoe."

I looked at Jack a bit puzzled. He seemed to pick up on my confusion.

"Comprehensive school, like your high school. Dad had started at University." I nodded and looked back to Elise to finish.

"My parents and I settled down at the end of the dock and cast out our lines. I was watching the three boys in the canoe not far from us. They were drifting closer, and the boy at the stern caught my eye. We watched each other over the lake for about an hour when I thought I had a bite. I stood up and began to reel my line in. At the same time, the boy in the boat stood up and was teetering back and forth on the canoe, struggling to reel his line in.

He was rocking the canoe back and forth and then lost balance and ended up in the lake. As it turned out, I had literally fished him out of the lake and into my heart. Our hooks had intertwined underwater."

"Hey Mom, tell her about the dream part, too." Jack came sauntering over to us and plopped down on the ottoman at my feet.

"Oh yes, the dream. You see it wasn't as easy as just hooking each other. James was pretty mad that our lines had woven together. He didn't see the amusement in it that I had. When he climbed up onto the dock soaking wet and set about untangling the lines, I couldn't stop giggling, partly because I was completely taken by this boy, but also because he looked pretty funny at that moment. I quietly introduced myself to him and watched him grumble back down the shoreline with his pole, waiting for his buddies to pick him up.

Well, that night, I had a dream. It must have been around the time of WW2. There was this girl, about my age, walking a dark street alone. She came across a set of army dog tags which had been wedged between two rocks in the burned out rubble of an old house. She put them in her pocket and took them to the army base. She found the boy they belonged to and was able to give them back to him. It was sweet really, but it made me want to go back to the lake to see if I could find him again. Sure enough, he was there, hoping I would show up again."

"And the rest, they say, is history." James was leaning on the kitchen counter, watching his wife retell their love story. They seemed to share a moment as their eyes connected knowingly. "She will tell you that we both dreamt to meet each other there, but I was just back there to look for the cap I had left on the shore."

"Stop spoiling all the fun, grumpy; you know you really came back to find me."

"Whatever you want to believe, my love." James bent down to kiss Elise, and I turned away, blushing.

Elise's dream made me think about not only Katherine and John, but Aunt Cathy and Uncle Bern, too.

"My aunt and uncle fell in love on this lake, too. Uncle Bern was living at his parents' cottage for the summer when Aunt Cathy came for a week with her family on vacation."

"Yeah Mum, it's funny, we just found a picture of them on the lake when they were about our age." Jack threw his arm around me which I ducked away from and shot him a look.

"This is a magical place. We left for a while and lived in London, got married, had Jack, and worked pretty mundane jobs. When Jack turned 10, we knew that we wanted more, so we bought this house and opened the market and haven't looked back since."

I was shocked at the dreamy look in James' eye and stifled a giggle. It was amazing to me the similarities in Elise and James' love and that of Aunt Cathy and Uncle Bern. It made me hopeful, but I knew that right now my life was too complicated for love.

I looked up to see Jack staring at me with a smile on his lips. I blushed and looked away completely annoyed, stifling the uncharacteristic, immature urge to stick out my tongue.

"So James, how did you learn to make all of those items in the bakery?" I said, changing the subject.

"My mum was a fantastic baker, she taught me well. Come on, I will show you all my secrets." We went back to the bakery where James and I made a batch of cinnamon rolls together. The quiet he offered was comforting and just what I needed. Lately my mind had been running rampant, and the dreams I had been having were beginning to wreck havoc. I was having more and more trouble shaking them. They were beginning to stay with me longer and longer into the day, which was both thrilling and worrisome.

That night as I lay in bed, I thought about all the love that was surrounding me lately- The Hollings family, Katherine and John in my dream, my aunt and uncle. I wanted to believe that this was my mom's way of sharing her love with me. I felt warmed by its embrace and a wonderful sense of peace, yet at the same time a great unease began to creep through it all, and I had no idea what to do with it. I wanted to stay in this little bubble of happiness that had enveloped my life. It felt safe and secure.

Chapter 5

The first thing I noticed was the smell of leaves, lifeless piles of leaves at the beginning stages of mildew. I was surrounded with trees in various stage of leaf ruin. Up ahead was a dusty path, and I almost ran for it, to escape the heavy tang in the air.

My feet hit the path at the same time I saw them just up ahead. I fell into step behind them, scrambling to put less distance between us so I could hear what they were whispering to each other. Farther up ahead, Becca was dragging a stick through the dirt and chattering away about this and that and who knew what else. She was so lost in her own little world that Katherine and John took the opportunity to grasp hands as they walked. Katherine tried to keep them concealed in the folds of her skirt. I could tell that this was not something new to them, perhaps something they did everyday on their walk home from school.

"Mama said the new preacher will be here by Sunday." Katherine seemed to be very excited, but John's mind appeared far away, and it didn't take long for Katherine to notice.

"Can I ask what is on your mind? You look lost in thought."

"I was just thinking about us, and what our future holds."

This immediately makes Katherine blush; she looked like she was going to drop his hand out of shock. This lasted a fraction of a second, and she was able to compose herself with a response.

"Well, isn't that a bit presumptuous of you, Mr. Cooper?" she shyly responded.

"Katherine, you and I both know that we were meant for each other. There is no need in hiding it or pretending it doesn't exist. I can't think about a future that doesn't include you in it. Why wouldn't I want to discuss it with you?"

Katherine dropped his hand just as Becca turned around to see what had caused John's voice to rise. It only lasted a moment before a little wren caught her attention.

"John, Pa says that I am too young, at 16, to be fancying myself after any boys. I know it is just because Ma needs my help, too." Katherine looked down at the ground, knowing that she had hurt his feelings and feeling ashamed herself. "Pa just isn't the same anymore. I'm so sorry. I don't think any of us know how to deal with him anymore."

John pulled himself to a stop and turned to face her. "Do you see me in your future?" he dejectedly forced out.

"Of course I do, of course. I can't picture anything without seeing you in it. But I can't go against Pa; that is why we have to be so careful. John, he will…" And she trailed off, still looking at the ground.

Becca broke the silence, running back to them, oblivious to their far too intimate exchange.

"Look what landed on my hand, Katherine, a butterfly. Oh, it tickles." Becca held out a beautiful, cerulean blue butterfly.

My eyes began to lose focus as I stared at the butterfly in her hand. It was the most beautiful color I have ever seen. Its wings were vibrant blue with thin black and white stripes running along the outer edge of each wing. The blue seemed to spread out, covering everything I could see. Then it all slowly began to fade, but Becca's high-pitched giggles of delight continued to ring in my ears.

As soon as I woke up, not wanting to miss the opportunity to capture the exquisiteness of the butterfly, I hopped out of bed and began to mix colors. I had to capture the exact cerulean shade of blue that covered the butterfly's wings. I spent about an hour perfecting the shade and placing the butterfly in the right spot on the painting. Since I didn't paint people, I decided to put the butterfly on a flower in Becca's little garden. It was the next best thing to placing it on her hand.

When I was satisfied with the results, I cleaned up and hopped in the shower. I had come to accept these strange story-like dreams as a part of life on Rudyard Lake. I couldn't explain why I was having them or what they meant; I had stopped trying to figure them out.

I was lost in my thoughts about John and Katherine. It was so hard to watch them hide their love. I wanted them to be able to be together and happy. It hurt my heart to watch them sometimes. I wanted to find peace but couldn't. It was similar to how I felt about my life recently. I knew my mom would want me to find peace in my life, but I couldn't allow myself to get there. The Hollings brought me some happiness and I welcomed it, yet something was still missing; I was yet to feel whole. I got out of the shower and tried to embrace the day.

Today I was cooking with Elise. I had been looking forward to it for a long time. Aunt Cathy and Uncle Bern were expected tomorrow, and we were going to make dinner for them. I was so excited to see them again, I had missed them so much, but I was even more excited to introduce them to the Hollings. My life had changed so much in the four weeks that I had been here, and I was so grateful that I had come. Aunt Cathy and Uncle Bern were staying for the next three weeks and then traveling back home with me. It was hard for me to think about returning to North Carolina, even though I knew it was inevitable.

Thoughts of Elise consumed my shower. Spending the whole day under her tutelage made me giddy with excitement. I even added a little makeup to my usually bland attire.

I arrived at the Market, a little early. The Hollings' house sat on the lake, just in front of the market. It was two houses that with some craftsmanship had been joined together. Jack and James were running the store today so Elise and I could cook. No one was up front, but the bell announced my arrival and James quickly came out from behind the bakery counter to greet me.

"Hey Ava, nice to see you." His eyes were warm and friendly. He didn't say much, but he really didn't have to; his eyes and smile spoke for him. He gave me a quick hug and told me Elise was waiting in the house for me, ushering me through the doorway that separated the market from the house. The hallway leading from the market to the house was lined with pictures of Jack at various ages. One picture caught my eye. Jack was sitting on a horse; he was probably 5. I am not sure why, but I was momentarily lost in that picture, consumed with thoughts I couldn't quite grasp. There was something familiar in his smile.

I came through the doorway to find Elise washing some dishes in the sink; she didn't hear my arrival. I didn't want to startle her, so I called softly from the doorway, "Hey Elise."

"Oh, Ava" she said cheerfully, wiping her hands on the dishtowel that hung from her apron string. "I'm so glad we get to spend the day together! I've been thinking all night about what we can make, and I think I have the perfect meal planned for us." Her smile radiated peace and home.

I could hear rustling coming from the couch and looked into the living room to see Jack's head pop up over the back of the couch.

"Bloody hell, can you two keep it down, I am trying to sleep." Jack plopped back down onto the couch with a "hrumph".

"Jack didn't sleep at all last night, insomnia I guess." Then she turned toward the couch and softly said, "Hey sleepy head, take yourself up to your room. Ava and I are going to get busy in here. And Dad will need your help a little later, but go get caught up on some sleep first."

Jack begrudgingly emerged from the couch, walking past me in a stupor as he headed for the stairs. He turned and stuck his tongue out at me on the way.

"Real mature, Jack." I smiled back at him.

I turned to Elise who was gathering materials and laying them on the counter. She turned on some music, and we began a very comfortable dance in the kitchen preparing shepherd's pie for dinner. Her skill in the kitchen was one of familiarity, comfort, and years of practice. I felt a little ill at ease. Although I had spent several years preparing meals for me and my mom, it was usually very simple things like macaroni and cheese or spaghetti, not elaborate meals with many ingredients. I enjoyed our time and didn't want it to end.

A part of me wanted to tell Elise about my dreams. I just couldn't find the words I needed, and every time I thought about it, my mouth wouldn't open to let the words out. It was as if something was stopping me. Perhaps it was the fact that dreams were unusual, strange, and I wasn't sure exactly how to explain them.

Spending time with Elise was so comfortable, but a part of me felt like I had to keep some things closed off, as if telling her about my inner secrets would void memories of my mom. Almost as if she could tell where my thoughts were, she brought my mom up in conversation.

"Did you and your mum cook together, dear?" She looked at me tentatively.

"No, Mom wasn't much of a cook." I smiled sheepishly at her, trying to stifle the tears that were creeping in.

"I'm sorry, is it too hard for you to talk about her? I would love to know more about her. She sounds like she was a great mum, and she certainly can be proud of the woman you are."

"Thank you. She was amazing, and I am proud to be her daughter. It is getting easier to think about her. It makes it easier being with you and James and Jack. I wish I wasn't leaving so soon. You remind me of her, a lot actually. You both always see the good in people."

"Well, Rudyard Kipling said, 'I always prefer to believe the best of everybody; it saves so much trouble.' I like to think that way."

At one point Elise sent me over to the market to get some oregano, and I watched Jack and James work in the bakery for a few moments. They were unaware of my presence, and I was able to see the similarities between the two. The structure of Jack's face was the same as James'. They shared the same deep set eyes, but Jack definitely had Elise's full mouth. I was somewhat aware of the look in Jack's eyes; he was far away in thought and didn't appear to be too happy at the moment. I chalked it up to his lack of sleep and headed back to the kitchen.

My phone was ringing when I entered the house. I had to fish it out of the couch cushions, but by the time I retrieved it no one was there. Looking at the number, I saw it was Aunt Cathy, and I immediately called her back.

"Ava, oh Ava, honey, Nana Murphy passed this morning."

"Oh no." I was frozen in place as immediately the realization hit me, and I insensitively burst out, "So you're NOT coming?" I regretted it as soon as I said it.

"Ava, sweetie. We are so sorry."

"No, no, I am the one that is sorry. What happened?"

As Aunt Cathy proceeded to tell me about the midnight phone call from the nursing home and the long ride there; I sat on the couch, completely frozen. Uncle Bern was devastated. I told her I could be on the next flight out, which of course she refused and said that Uncle Bern insisted that I not come home, that his mother would not have wanted me to miss my last few weeks there, especially since they knew that I was enjoying my time so much.

It was hard to take it all in, and she had to get off the phone to tend to details but promised to call me back a little later. I sat for a long time on the couch stuck in a suspended space of thought. Elise came over and sat on the couch next to me and took my hand but let me sit in silence until I was ready.

"They're not coming", was all I could say; it was all I could allow myself to think at the moment. If I let my mind loose, my emotions would have a field day.

"What can we do, sweetheart?"

"Just sit with me for a minute. I have to think of what to do." And as a burst in the dam, it all tumbled out.

"My Uncle Bern's mother died. They don't want me to come home early, but I feel like I have to. I don't know what to do.

Death, more death." I buried my face in my hands and gave in to the tears.

Elise rubbed my back and did the best thing that she could have done at that moment: she said nothing, sensing that I wasn't ready for any questions.

I didn't know Nana Murphy very well. She had been in a nursing home for years. Uncle Bern went to see her twice a month, but I hadn't seen her since I was about 7. I wanted to ask my mom what she thought I should do, and this brought about another round of tears. I couldn't put my finger on what she would want me to do, or my mind wouldn't let me think about it. I wasn't sure which one as a part of me wanted to believe that my mom would tell me to go home. I didn't want to leave, wasn't ready to say goodbye to my new family, and couldn't even think about having to say goodbye to them in three weeks as it was.

Jack came in through the kitchen and saw Elise on the couch with me and my face still in my hands.

"What's wrong?" He stood behind the couch with a look of fear on his face.

"Bern's mother died." Elise quietly told him.

"So they aren't coming?" This had been Jack's first reaction, too, which made me feel a tiny bit better. He came around and sat down on the other side of me.

"Oh gee, Ava, I am sorry." And then the realization hit him and the look of fear returned to his face.

"Does this mean you are leaving early?" His eyes widened, and I couldn't help but smile at him as I knew the awareness was hitting him as hard as it hit me.

"My uncle doesn't want me to. I don't think I do either, but the feeling of guilt is overwhelming me right now."

And in typical Jack fashion, he grabbed my knee and said "Well, you don't have to decide right this minute. Dad's letting me knock off early. How about coming down to the boat with me? It's almost done."

His hand on my knee tickled, and I had to lift it away. Looking at his face brought me such peace, yet I couldn't figure out exactly why. Maybe it was because he was always so positive and good-natured. Without even thinking I hugged Elise and started to get up off of the couch. Jack grabbed my hand and kept a hold of it as we walked out toward the lake. He didn't say anything until we got to the boat he was building.

"OK, Ms. Banks, I know you don't like the water, so why don't you sit on that log over there and watch the master at work?" He pointed to a log standing upright with a perfect seat carved out of the top. I smiled as I knew that Jack had carved out the seat.

While I sat on the log, he commanded my attention with stories of each part of the boat and how he had put it all together. This lasted for about 20 minutes, just the perfect amount of time to calm my mind. He came to sit down next to me. We both looked out over the lake for awhile, catching a gull midflight with something long and floppy hanging out of its mouth.

"It's OK to feel guilty, but you know your Uncle is right. He knows that you are still grieving for your own mom and this is the place you need to be right now."

"Thank you, Jack, I appreciate that. I am most upset about them not coming, and of course I feel guilty about that, too."

"Don't let guilt make you do something you will later regret. Come on, I know just what you need." Jack grabbed my hand and propelled us down to the lake. He steered us around the bend on the lake and right down to the train station before I could even process what he was doing.

Jack paid for my ticket, settled me in the front seat, and then took the seat behind me. I looked back over my shoulder at him and had to stifle a giggle; he looked so proud of himself. He knew the train ride was important to me and was actually just what I needed at that moment.

As we rode the train in silence, I thought about my mom and just let the good memories come. The train whistle emphasized my memories and helped to put my mind back into focus. Everything happens for a reason; we may not always like what happens, but we have to find the message in the bottle, so to speak. I was desperately trying to find the message all of this was sending to me. The dreams, the dashed hopes I had for Aunt Cathy and Uncle Bern's visit, my feelings for Elise and James, and the confusing feelings I had for Jack. I turned to look at him as the train made its way back to the station. His arm was propped up on the side of the seat, his face resting in his palm. His face was serene as he looked out over the lake he loved so much. Jack Hollings always seemed to know exactly what I needed. He turned to face me, and the look we shared sent chills down my back, yet I couldn't look away.

"Thank you," was all I said. Jack winked at me in return.

When the train came back to the station, Jack once again grabbed my hand and we walked back to his house in silence. His hand felt heavy in mine and felt very strange, but I was too emotionally drained and needed the extra comfort. I was too confused to fight my feelings for him today. I needed them to be just what they were, for now.

We sat outside talking for a little while longer. At some point Aunt Cathy called and we talked more about the arrangements. Uncle Bern and I spoke for a bit, and he emphatically told me to stay where I was and enjoy the lake. It had been his mother's favorite place, and it made him happy to know I was there and having a good time. This made me feel better, even though I was still sad about not getting to introduce them to the Hollings.

We all agreed that I would still come home the first week of August as planned, but that they would not be coming out. Uncle Bern had to take care of all of the arrangements as he was the only son, and he also had to take care of emptying out her little space at the home.

Jack walked me home, one hand holding the bag of leftovers Elise had packed for me, the other firmly holding onto my hand. We didn't say anything as we walked, but we didn't need to. Everything that needed to be said was found, once again, in his firm grasp. There was a flickering of something in the trees off the lane that caught my eye. It was a butterfly that seemed to be following us. My mind went back to my dream and the blue butterfly that landed on Becca's hand, and this thought brought me comfort.

The butterfly was a reminder that there was something greater than myself out there watching over me. I was beyond exhausted and couldn't wait to get home and hopefully dream of my happy little family in the woods. The only words Jack spoke as he left me at the door were, "Sleep well." He seemed just as lost in thought as I did.

I lay in bed with my hands under my pillows and stared at my painting. I had an uneasy feeling that it was all going to disappear and be gone like my mom and Nana Murphy. I stared at the butterfly, hoping to make sense of it all.

The dim light of the lantern blurred in my vision as I tried to take in the tiny room I was standing in. The table was being cleared from supper, and Pa was sitting in the rocking chair smoking a pipe, a sour look on his face. It was unusually quiet. Gabriel's face was tense as he ran a cloth over the table. The girls were in the kitchen talking in hushed tones so that I couldn't make out what they were saying. The smell of the pipe churned my stomach and flooded my head with memories that I couldn't quite reach.

I felt the tension building as the girls carefully edged around the room, avoiding the rocking chair. The fire was casting strange shadows on the walls, giving the room an eerie glow.

"Katherine, it is time for your studies," Ma whispered.

"I just have to grab my books from the loft." Katherine disappeared up the ladder to her room and emerged a few minutes later with two books. She sat at the table and began nervously reading, her fingers running along the edge of her teeth.

Gabriel sat down at the far end of the table closest to where I stood. Even though his books were open in front of him, his eyes were all over the room, particularly on Becca who was now crouched in the corner playing with a doll.

"Boy, run out to the barn and get me my switch," Pa mumbled from the chair.

"Yes, Pa." Gabriel looked up at Katherine and then Becca and their eyes shared a mutual fear; who was going to get it tonight, and why?

Katherine and Becca glanced around nervously as Ma retreated to the kitchen, not meeting their eyes. Gabriel returned and tentatively handed the switch to Pa.

Pa began, gently stroking the long leather strap, "Katherine, how long have you been seeing Johnny Cooper?"

"What? Um, oh Pa, I see him every day at school." Katherine swallowed, and the tears were threatening her eyes.

"Haven't I told you enough that you are not to be seeing that boy?"

"But Pa, we are friends. You were friends with his Pa. We are family." Katherine sat up a little straighter in her chair.

"That's enough out of you. You do not have time to fancy yourself after boys. Your studies and work for your mother are

more important than anything else. You and Johnny Cooper are no longer friends. Do you understand what I am saying to you?" His voice was booming off the wooden walls.

"Yes, Pa." Katherine hung her head in defeat.

Becca watched Katherine from the corner, cuddling her doll in her arms. I could very faintly hear her whispering to the doll, "There, there, settle down now. You are OK."

Pa fondled the switch in his hand as if he were contemplating her punishment. Katherine didn't take her eyes off of him, almost daring him to use it. I marveled at her bravery. Pa looked up and caught her defiant gaze which made her drop her eyes immediately.

My heart ached for her. I could feel the quickness of her heartbeat within my chest and the anguish that tortured her mind. She was trying desperately to stifle the running thoughts that were struggling to take hold.

Pa's booming voice made me jump. "If I find out that you are seeing him outside of school, this switch will become your worst nightmare." Pa grumbled and stood from the chair, lost in thought. He retreated outside and staggered a bit to the barn.

When the door slammed shut, sending reverberations through the cabin, I could hear the collective expulsion of air from the three children. Katherine's eyes were holding back the tears and I could taste them in my throat.

Ma emerged from the kitchen with a pie and placed it gingerly on the table. She stood straight, clapped her hands and produced a large smile at her children. "Look at what I have for dessert, a fresh blueberry pie, thanks to our darling blueberry picker, Rebecca!"

The three just stared at Ma while she busied herself cutting slices of the pie. She chattered away, something about the plumpest blueberries, as the children gaped at her in stunned silence.

I felt the shame rise in my cheeks, shame for this mother so lost in her own hell that she could not bring herself to admit it to herself or her children. I knew deep down that she couldn't do anything but try to make it all disappear; she was powerless over her husband. Somehow I don't think that the three children could comprehend what I was able to see. The confusion on Becca's face as she squeezed the doll tightly in her arms spoke for all of them.

I wanted to follow Pa but wasn't sure how to get out the door. Could I just walk through the wall? Somehow I doubted this. I edged closer to the window and caught sight of Pa standing just outside the barn, still smoking his pipe.

He was kicking up dust with his boots, his free hand
tangled in his hair. Concentrating on his face, I thought I saw
tears running down his cheeks, but from this distance it was hard
to tell. The dust cloud began to rise, and I was lost to the sea of
dirt and brown.

I woke with my hands over my eyes, trying to shield them from the emerging dust. It was too early in the morning, and when I realized where I was, the dream still hanging on in my brain. I didn't move as I wanted to hold the memories long enough to make sense of them.

Poor Katherine and Gabriel. Becca too. The terror and confusion that their father brought them still clung to my chest. My mind was a jumble of emotions as I recalled the dream I had earlier about their father, obviously at a happier time when he and John's father harvested their crops together. What had happened to this confident man that had reduced him to an angry, selfish shell that would beat his children and terrify his family?

I just couldn't shake the feeling that Pa had once been the life of the family, a gentle protector and provider, but I couldn't grasp what could have caused him to turn on them in such a way. The tears started to roll onto my pillow as visions of my mom took over the strained memories of the dream.

I silently thanked my mom for being both mother and father and raising me the best that she could and with love and generosity. Many times throughout my life I had asked my mom about my father, but all the information that I ever got from her was that he wasn't around and never would be. Aunt Cathy told me once that he disappeared when he found out my mom was pregnant and they had never heard from him again. I never understood why mom wouldn't ever give me any information about him, not even his name. The more I asked, the more upset she would get about it. Once, my senior year in high school, I broke down to Aunt Cathy and she confided in me that my mom wasn't sure exactly who my father was. I stopped asking after that and decided I didn't want to know.

I hated mornings when I woke up crying and full of grief and emotion. I gave myself the time to cry and talk to my mom and feel the loss and helplessness, something that I had become very good at doing. Something about being at Rudyard Lake made it a little bit easier to confront my feelings. Something far away, yet close enough to envelope me, helped me to begin to deal with them. Yet emotions were never easy to handle, especially grief.

Just when things had been going so well, these emotions crept back in. I couldn't distinguish between my own grief and concern for Katherine. The waters were muddied, distorting my own thoughts. It was as if a switch was being flipped back and forth in my brain, turning off and on various emotions which I had no control over.

I spent most of the morning in bed alternating between grieving for my mom and contemplating Katherine's family and their plight. Both thoughts entwined in helpless emotion. Just when things seemed to be going so well, the bottom fell out and all I was left with was the vast stretch of thoughts as I tried to grab onto something that made sense.

At some point in the day, after dodging texts from Jack urging me to come help him with the campers and forcing myself to half-heartedly paint or read I took a fretful nap.

I was standing in a small crowd of people dressed in their very best. I noticed at once that my usual attire was replaced with a light blue dress dotted with small flowers, and a large bow was hanging across my shoulders from the back of my braided hair. I didn't have to look at Katherine to know that she was dressed the same way.

I noticed all of the familiar faces. Katherine holding on to Becca's hand, Gabriel next to her kicking at the muddy earth with his boot. Ma was standing slightly behind Pa with her head hung low. All of them were crying, and I noticed that tears were also running down my face.

Squinting my eyes, I tried to make out the other faces in the group. Across the muddy path were John and his mother, holding hands and softly crying as they stared at the plain brown coffin being lowered into the ground. I immediately knew who lay inside that box even though I had no idea how I knew this or why John's pa was being laid to rest.

I watched Pa's face carefully and could almost see his grief change him, harden him. But why? I had to know what happened and was determined to stay in this dream until I found out. I was stricken with a sickening feeling that I wouldn't like what I found out.

No one spoke as I followed them into the house; everyone's eyes turned to the ground. I wanted to scream at them for someone to tell me what had happened.

Once inside the house all they could do was cry and hug. Both mothers turned their shared grief into food for the family while the children huddled around each other sharing their emotions. Only Pa was absent, gone out to barn where he would stay. I stole my way into the tiny kitchen, hoping to uncover what had happened as Ma spoke softly.

"Mary Alice, you know that we will do whatever we can to help you and Johnny. You are the closest thing to family we have out here."

"Thank you so much. I don't know how we will manage without him. Poor Albert, I wish he would talk to us. I can't imagine what he is feeling right now. He won't even listen or look at me when I try to talk to him."

"He will come around. I know he is blaming himself, but he also knows that Peter wouldn't want him to, and the only thing he would want him to do is to help you and Johnny. They were best friends, like brothers, and my Albert will do the right thing, I know he will."

"I wish he wouldn't blame himself. It was an accident. Oh Janie, what are we going to do? Johnny will have to drop out of school and he will never be able to get the crops planted."

Ma wrapped her arms around Mary Alice. "We will make it work. I promise you."

As Ma and Mary Alice swayed together, my tears blurred my eyes.

I woke to the light streaming in through the window. It was late afternoon, but the clock was blinking 11:17. At some point while I napped the power must have gone out and come back on again. It was almost as if time had suspended while I slept. I felt a shift in everything as I reset the clock to the correct time, resenting the number which was now mocking me as it blinked off and on. This number had a strange way of popping up, and I wasn't sure I liked it.

I felt unsettled, as if something bad was lurking around the corner. The only certain thought that ran through my mind was that something bad had happened between Albert and Peter. It didn't sit well with me as the story was still filled with too many holes.

Chapter 6

August seemed so close, and I began to feel some urgency in my days. My few tender moments with Jack and the fact that I was leaving so soon brought a new, complex emotion: How did I feel about leaving Jack? What were my feelings for him? I had trouble allowing these emotions to the surface as I was most afraid of reliving the feelings of grief that were still too familiar to me in the wake of my mom's death. I could feel it changing me, hardening me.

Jack had so quickly become an important person in my life, and this confused and terrified me. I couldn't imagine my life without him, yet I knew that I wasn't ready to let him in completely. Jack had provided me with humor and friendship, both of which I had been lacking for so long. The irony was that it was all about to be ripped away from me, creating an all too familiar rawness that I was trying so hard to protect myself from ever feeling again. Part of me knew that I was in too deep, and the drowning waters were forcing me to think quickly, react too fast. My mind was in a constant state of "jumbling," and I didn't like it. I had never liked feeling that way, even when I was in school and had trouble concentrating and focusing on the lessons. It was almost too much for my mind to sort through. This is how it felt now as I tried to navigate through the mess my mind was creating.

This feeling scared me as I felt I was slowly slipping back into the murky waters that filled my mind after my mom's death. How quickly things were changing, reminding me that life was like the ocean, one moment calm and inviting, and the next turbulent and troubled.

Grief is a wretched emotion. It drains every speck of raw feeling that lives in your thoughts. My emotions of the last 24 hours mixed with the emotions left over from the dream created a miserable morning. Everything seemed to terrify me, and I wasn't sure which way I should move. I was scared of losing my grip on the happiness that I had found here in England, scared of what the next few months would hold for me. The fear of telling Aunt Cathy and Uncle Bern of my thwarted college plans and the uncertainty of what I was going to do mixed with the irrational fear I had for Katherine, Becca and Gabriel at the hands of their father. The loss that they all felt over John's pa's death mixed with my own lingering grief of my loss swirled in my head.

It was just a dream, but was also carried so deep in my heart that I couldn't distinguish between what was real and what was imaginary anymore. I wanted so desperately to cling to the sweetness of this place and the Hollings family but at the same time felt the sting of Pa's switch at the thought of leaving them. I felt the heaviness of death that was now melding reality with my dreams.

Why had I allowed myself to get so close to the Hollings, when just like everything else it would have to end? I thought that I might welcome the sting of the switch over the sting of the loss. The thought of going home and grieving for the distance between me and the Hollings terrified me. I had to put some distance between me and them, lessen the pain. Although I tried to get some space from them, I just found it nearly impossible to do without hurting them, which scared me even more. The harder I tried, the more grief I felt, and I found myself pulling away even more.

I decided to paint my grief. I set up a new canvas in my room and settled down with a cup of coffee, a cinnamon bun, and my paints. I was supposed to spend the day with Jack, helping him with his boat, but I just couldn't bring myself to leave the house today. Some days emotions just enveloped me, and I had to hold on for dear life until it passed. My mom's death, Nana's death, leaving Rudyard Lake, Katherine's pa, Katherine and John, it was all too much for me to hold onto and something had to change, yet I felt powerless to change any of it.

While I painted, my mind was wandering all over the place. I settled on a particularly strange memory of my mom. We were living in Aunt Cathy's basement at the time. I was about 7 and was in the corner playing with my Barbies. I overheard my mom's conversation with Aunt Cathy, but at the time I couldn't make much sense of it. The words still surfaced every once in awhile though.

"I am afraid that I am losing it, Cath."

"You are not losing it, Liz, you are just going through a rough time, and it will all be OK."

"There are times that I think my head is going to explode. How can I afford all the things that I want to give to Ava? You and Bern are too good to me, but I want to earn it myself."

"Stop looking at the big picture, Lizzy. Just take one day at a time and you and Ava will make it. I promise you."

Aunt Cathy's words, "Stop looking at the big picture," echoed in my head. I think I am a lot like my mom in that way. I always think too far ahead, try to think about too much at once, analyze every little detail. My poor mom always tried so hard to make life perfect for me. If she only realized that it was perfect; it was the only life I knew, and I was happy. More than anything I wish that I could tell her that my life had always been happy. I like to think that she knew that.

I tried to remember that and also tried not to look at the big picture. If I focused too much on what hadn't happened yet, I could get lost in the anxiety of it all. It was a daily struggle, but I was trying. Painting helped. Focusing on just one part of the picture and then working my way out in different directions at a time, a picture would start to emerge. It felt good to concentrate on one small detail at a time. Why couldn't I do that with my life?

It had been about five days since I had seen him, and sure enough Jack came knocking at the door in a surly mood.

"Ava, where are you?" he called through the window.

"In here, painting."

"Where have you been? You don't answer my calls, and you haven't even texted me back. What gives?"

"Oh, I have been busy, took a trip into Leek for the day." Noticing his pained expression, I continued quickly, "and I've been painting a lot, too. I have to finish this before I leave, and I am working on another one I want to finish as well."

"Well, you are coming out with me Saturday night. A few of us are having a bonfire out on the lake, and you can't miss it."

"I don't know Jack, I kinda just feel like staying in."

"Come on, you haven't been out in days. You have to go!"

"No, I don't have to go, I mean, I am not your girlfriend." I wanted to take it back the minute I said it, and I had to look away from his hurt face. "I'm sorry, that was rude. I just don't feel like being sociable right now."

"No, I get it. That's OK, you can just stay in here and wallow away in your misery." I let that one go, partly because I had just taken a jab at him and partly because I knew he was right.

"OK, OK, I will go, but just for a little bit. I just can't keep getting attached to you and your family; it isn't right." I looked down at my feet shyly.

"I know, I know, because you are leaving in just a few weeks, blah blah. I don't care, Ava, we are already attached. It's a little too late for that. Don't for one minute think that I am going to forget about you when you leave. Mum and I have already been talking about a trip across the pond before Christmas."

"Really? Wow, just to see me?"

"Well, that, and to shop in New York." Jack punched my arm and forced a smile from me.

I felt a little better. I didn't know how Jack kept weaseling his way in, but a part of me was secretly glad. I had had enough of sitting around in my own grief, and even though a part of me was fighting it, I knew I couldn't stay away from him for too long. After hearing that he intended to stay in touch, it was easier for me to give in as well.

"I have to head down to the sailing club. Come on with me."

"Not today, Jack. I want to finish a painting I have been working on. I said I will go with you on Saturday." I think he could sense the exhaustion in my voice and backed off a bit.

"Ok, I'll let you be. As long as I know you are OK. I've been worried about you." He tousled my hair, unnerving me a bit.

"I'm OK Jack, really. Just been a bit emotional this week." I wanted to tell him about Katherine and John, but it all sounded so silly in my head.

"Well, you know how to reach me if you need me." He looked like he was going to lean down and kiss me, which made me back away a bit on the couch. A shock went through me which scared me even more.

After Jack left, I threw myself into finishing my painting, not wanting to give too much thought to my conversation with Jack. My mind just wasn't ready to deal with my feelings for him and I was happy to push them away.

I spent the rest of the afternoon finishing up the painting from my dream. The butterfly ended up being the central focal point of the painting. It looked like it could fly right off the canvas, its brilliant blue in such sharp contrast to the muted colors of its surroundings. I fell asleep looking at it perched atop a patch of wildflowers in the tiny garden. My thoughts were on Jack, and as much as I tried not to think about him, my mind just went right back to him, trying so hard not to think about how much I would miss him when I left.

I could hear Gabriel's laughter as I emerged from the tree line. Heading toward the barn to investigate, I almost stumbled over a stump in the path, sending the toe of my boot through my skirt hem, ripping a large hole. I shook my head at the cumbersome mess of material that hung heavily down my legs.

As I rounded the corner of the barn, I could see Becca sitting on the floor right in the middle of the barn, awash in sunlight. She was peering into a small, wooden bucket and squealing with delight. Gabriel stood over her. I walked closer toward them, still somewhat uncomfortable with the fact that they had no idea that I was there.

Peering over Gabe's shoulder, I could see three small, yellow puff balls in the basket- newborn chicks.

"I'm calling this one Sunshine. This one will be Buttercup. I haven't thought of a name for the third one yet." She peered up at Gabe.

"How 'bout Supper?" Gabe said jokingly.

Becca didn't like his joke and grabbed the bucket up with the three small chicks inside and ran out the barn, calling for Katherine.

I stood and watched Gabe for awhile as he was lost in thought, a painful look in his eyes. Pa came around the corner and barked out Gabe's name, causing him to jump.

"Coming, Pa." He took off in a run, gliding to a stop in front of his father.

The man and son strode off into the sunlight, leaving me alone in the barn, listening to the animal noises around me. Just as I was about to leave, Katherine came through the large front opening, tears streaming down her cheeks. I followed her up the ladder to the second floor and sat down on a hay pile opposite her. She wiped at her tears, only to be replaced by more. She hung her head in her hands, and I wanted to reach out and stroke her hair, telling her it would all be OK. Katherine's sorrow beat out in my own heart, her tears stung my eyes.

Noise below startled me, and gathering my skirt in my hands, I leaned over the rickety railing to investigate. The streaming sun blocked my view of the door. I raised my hand to shield my eyes and could make out John as he entered the shadows farther inside the barn. I could tell that another figure was leaning against the doorjamb but couldn't make out who was lost in the shadow.

John searched around the barn, scanning each animal pen and hay pile. "Katherine, please come out," he called into the shadows. His eyes scanned the loft, and a smile threatened his lips. He moved toward the ladder, and the figure behind him moved out of the light, forcing me to gasp and cover my mouth *with my hand. I immediately crouched down and moved back into the hay.*

My thoughts were racing as my eyes darted around the loft. I crouched down farther and peered through the small slat of the railing. I couldn't believe what I was seeing. It was so misplaced, like seeing a dark grey cloud on a bright sunny day. My mind was reeling; this couldn't be happening. It was so wrong.

Standing below me, just on the edge of the dusty, light line that painted the floor was Jack Hollings. I had to blink a few times and rub my eyes to make sure I was seeing what I was seeing. He didn't belong here. My heart was beating out of my chest, and I was having trouble catching my breath.

Instinctively I backed away from the railing just as John reached the top of the ladder. He looked around the room, his eyes coming to rest on Katherine, who still sat with her head in her hands. As he moved silently over to Katherine and sat down next to her, I moved back closer to the edge, trying to figure out why Jack would be ascending the ladder in my dream.

As Jack reached the top and stood up straight, his eyes caught mine, and we both gasped. He could see me, our eyes locked and not really knowing why, I moved my finger to my lips. Looking Jack up and down, I noticed that he was dressed exactly like John, the same faded brown overalls, blue shirt, and brown derby. I could tell that he was also appraising my gauche clothes. He covered his mouth stifling a giggle.

Katherine's sobs forced us to look in her direction.

"John, you have to leave. If Pa catches you here…" she broke off with more sobs.

"Shhh, your Pa and Gabe are long gone over the hill with the team. Stop crying and look at me. It is going to be OK; we will figure out something."

"NO John, we won't figure anything out. In a week you will be gone, and I may never see you again; the thought is unbearable."

"Kat, I will come back for you. Omaha isn't that far off, and once Ma is settled…" He paused, looking around the barn, his tears threatening, too.

"Oh John, stop, you know that once you leave here, you will not be able to return. You are going to work on the railroad, and your ma will need you."

Katherine tried desperately to regain herself as she stood and wiped at her face with the backs of her hands.

"Just go John, make it easier on both of us. Pa won't allow us to be together anyway and you need to go make a life for

yourself and take care of your ma." She tried her best to be strong but sunk back to the hay dejectedly.

John got down on his knees in front of her and grabbed her face in her hands. "I will be back for you as soon as you turn 18. I give you my promise, and my life." He lowered his lips to hers and their kiss consumed the space, causing Jack and I to look away from this most endearing display.

When I tried to look back, all I could see was Jack. He was staring at me as if he was seeing a ghost. I couldn't make it out either. What would he be doing here? I tried to say something, but no words came. Anything that I tried to say was drowned out by Katherine's sobs.

Shaking his head and not looking back at me, Jack walked over to John and stood behind him. It looked like he was ready to support him, help him up from the ground. John heaved a sigh and stood up straight, Jack right behind him.

"I will be back for you, my Katherine. I am doing this for us, so we can have a life together when you are 18. Nothing will keep me from coming back for you." It was as if John was more assured of himself with Jack standing behind him.

I stood watching them, my mouth gaping open, my mind in a flurry of thoughts mixed with Katherine's emotions. I looked around the loft, trying to find something to steady myself.

When I looked back, it was all gone. Katherine, John, and Jack had vanished as the light from the window bleached everything.

The light streaming in through the bedroom window illuminated my eyes even before I opened them. I didn't want to open them because then I would have to face my dream. It clung to the inside of my mind like the last drops of honey to the bottom of the jar.

Before I opened my eyes, I threw the sheet over my face. Under the covers I finally opened them and stared at the blurry teeny flower prints that shaded my eyes. Jack Hollings was in my dream, dressed as John. What on earth did that mean? My first reaction was annoyance; he didn't belong in my dreams, my private, personal story. But just as the teeny flowers began to focus and take definite shape before me, the thought dissolved into the recesses of my brain. I tried to keep hold of it, but like sand through my fingers it was gone from my mind.

I sat up, trying to piece everything together, which was becoming harder the more I woke up. John was leaving Katherine. I couldn't shake the certainty of this and the overwhelming need to scream as one more shadow of loss assailed my life. I shook my head trying to blot out any thought of my dream, trying to set myself back on reality and the choices I had to make about my life.

John and Katherine's life would have to wait; my life was getting too messy, and somehow I had to figure things out. Wasn't that what I had come here to do? The last of my lingering thoughts dissipated gently as my phone blared on the table, a text message from Jack.

What was that?

I blinked a few times, rereading the message. Annoyed again, I ignored the message and went about my morning routine, my thoughts fluctuating between John and Katherine and what I was going to do when I had to leave in two weeks.

Katherine was so distraught, and that feeling clung to me as did the sadness she faced at John's leaving. Her grief seemed to live inside me; I understood her emotion, this heart wrenching sense of loss. It beat out in my heart.

My phone blared again.

Ava, where are you?

Aggravated, I picked up the phone and answered him back curtly.

I am here, Jack

He didn't respond, which suited me just fine. I decided I was going to finish the painting today in honor of Katherine and John. I took a cinnamon roll and coffee up to my room and settled in front of the canvas. I wanted to add some more detail to the background, and then it should be finished. As with most of my paintings, I begin with the focal point and work my way out from there. It wasn't something I had ever been taught, it was just kind of how I did things. I was lost in thought when I heard the gasp behind me. I swung around to see Jack with his mouth hung open, staring at the painting.

"What are you doing here?"

"Ava, we have to talk." He walked over to the bed and sat down, never taking his eyes off of the painting.

"What is wrong with you? Come on Jack, I am getting tired of your theatrics."

"I've been there."

"What are you talking about, Jack?"

"I was there, too, Ava, in that dream."

"Where?"

"In my dream."

I had no reply; we sat and stared at each other as the realization sank in for both of us. I had sort of forgotten that I had seen Jack in my dream. It was lost to Katherine's grief that still lingered in my heart.

I don't know who asked the first question, they just seemed to fly out of both of us.

"You WERE in my dream last night?"

"I can't believe it was really you."

"How can we have dreamt the same thing?"

"What does this mean?"

"Wait a minute, this can't possibly be right." I wanted to bring some logic back in. "Hold on, let me ask the questions. I was in your dream too?"

"Yes! We dreamt the same thing."

"How can that possibly be? Jack this is insane. It must have been some coincidence or something. This just doesn't happen."

"How long have you been dreaming about Katherine?"

"Since I got here. Why?" It just didn't feel right, Jack saying her name.

"Ava, I have been dreaming about John off and on for years, since I was about 10, not long after we moved to the Lake."

"What is going on? Jack, this is insane."

"I'm not making this up, Ava. I am just as freaked out about this as you are."

We spent the better part of the morning comparing notes about our dreams. As it turned out, he had seen everything I had and more. He told me about the dreams he had as a child. I was completely mesmerized by these stories that felt even more personal now that I knew more about John. I could tell that Jack was as immersed in John's life as I had become in Katherine's, even more since he had spent so many years with John. And just when I didn't think I could take anymore, he told me about Peter's death.

"I was probably 15 at the time. I had just met Katherine with John at their school and felt the love between them immediately. Katherine would often walk Gabe home and then head over to John's house where she would greet her pa and John's pa as they finished up in the fields and then Pa would give her a ride home with the team. It was a very happy time.

"Her pa was jovial and kind and had an obvious friendship with Peter. I loved these dreams and couldn't wait to spend more time with them. John and Katherine were inseparable, and while they were still young they had a very easy way with each other.

"Then it all fell apart. Albert and Peter were working in the fields together as usual, and Albert loved to joke around while they worked while Peter was more serious. Katherine and John were running through the unusually tall wheat crops. They were probably 14 at the time. Peter was yelling at them to stop trampling down the crops and get back to the house, but they weren't listening. Peter was distracted trying to find them.

"Albert kept calling to him to let them go; they were just kids having fun. He was on one side of the horse team swinging his scythe in a rhythmic motion, humming to himself, when Peter came from around the front of the horses and caught the tip of the blade of Albert's scythe right across his neck."

Jack stopped there, seeing the horror on my face, but I urged him to keep going. I wanted to know every detail.

"It was complete chaos. I ran to Peter, completely helpless. Albert was wailing and calling for John and Katherine to run and get Mary Alice or Janie. He was completely out of control, and I couldn't do anything. I tried so hard to do something, but every time I tried to touch Peter, to stop the bleeding, it was like I was trying to tape a cloud. When Mary Alice got there, Albert told her that Peter ran into the scythe when it was propped up on the back of the cart. Seeing the anguish in his face as he told the lie was worse than seeing the actual death."

I put up my hand to Jack letting him know that I had heard enough. Katherine's pa had killed John's pa and then lied about it. The impossibility of those two thoughts sent me spinning. Pa had snapped; it was all starting to make sense now. He couldn't deal with the guilt and all the emotions he was feeling. But what he did to his family as a result was unthinkable. He had once been a happy father, farming alongside his best friend to provide for their families. His behavior after Peter's death now made more sense to me, why he didn't want Katherine and John together and why he was so surly all the time. My heart ached for him.

We spent the rest of the day processing all of it, which was kind of like asking someone to make sense of a hurricane blowing the contents of his house away. Where do you even begin? I told him about the dream I had where Pa threatened Katherine with the switch. He told me about John laboring by himself in the fields trying to harvest the wheat. Neither one of us could make sense of it.

What was even more perplexing was the fact that we both were dreaming about the same people. I was having a harder time dealing with it than Jack was. I still wasn't ready to share this with him, yet he seemed to know so much more than I did, and I wanted to know everything I could about each of them.

Jack spoke about them as if they were real, like he knew them. Even though I had felt that way about Katherine and her family, I still thought of them as just very vivid dreams and hadn't really tried to make sense of it, until now. I decided that mixing paints and easing brush strokes into clouds and trees and flowers was the only way to deal with it.

Jack and I talked while I finished the painting; he even added a few details that I had forgotten about, like the small creek that ran just behind the house. It could just be made out amongst the trees. When I was finished, we hung it on the wall opposite the bed so that I could look at it from where I slept. I was completely happy with it- it was the first thing that I had painted that did not come from a picture or a view I had while painting.

Jack and I lay on my bed and stared at the picture, both of us completely shocked by the recent developments. It was like we were discussing a movie we had both seen.

"Oh my, Jack. Do you think that somehow maybe, like we knew them or something?"

"I think we WERE them."

I sat up on the bed, "What are you saying? Like reincarnation or something?"

"I don't know, maybe? Tell me this, do you feel drawn to Katherine, like connected to her in some way? Do you feel what she is feeling, in here?" He gently touched his heart.

"Since the first dream, it's like I know what she is thinking without even thinking about it. Does that make sense?"

"Perfect sense. I have thought that about John for a long time, like I knew him, completely knew him. I always thought it was my mind's way of, I don't know, creating a movie about me, but it's not me." Jack pointed to the butterfly. "That is the butterfly that Becca caught." he said matter of factly.

"So why didn't I see you in that dream then? Why is it that we were only in the same dream with each other last night, yet I have had other dreams with John?"

"I don't know, maybe we dream the same thing at different times, and this was one time we collided." He gave a little chuckle, like he was kind of amused with himself.

"I wonder what will happen when I leave."

"I don't want to talk about that."

"It's inevitable, Jack."

"Yeah, I know, but right now I just want to think about today."

He turned over, and his eyes melted into mine. He leaned over and very gently kissed my lips. It was like a bolt of electricity ran through me, all the way to my legs. I wanted to push him away, but my brain and my arms were just not communicating correctly.

I was keenly aware of the fact that we were lying on my bed, and while the kiss made me feel alive, laying here with him felt wrong. I forced myself to jump up off the bed, blushing a little bit.

"Jack, I would rather not."

Jack sat up on his elbows and watched me squirm with a little smile on his face.

"It's OK, I understand. But can I just say, WOW."

I picked up a pillow and threw it at him.

"Come on, let's go eat. I am starving." I wanted to put as much distance between me and Jack and the bed as possible.

"So are you over avoiding me now?"

"I don't know, maybe not if you kiss me like that again."

I started for the step, not wanting to continue this conversation. Kissing Jack would NOT help me leave him in a few weeks, but I couldn't wipe the smile off of my face or get rid of the feelings it had given me.

"Hey, let's go invade Mum's fridge." Jack bounded down the steps, grabbed my hand, and pulled me toward the door.

We practically ran all the way to his house, and I let the gentle breeze wash away my worries. I loved being with Jack and his family and really truly wanted to make the best of my final weeks, as long as he didn't kiss me again I kept thinking.

Chapter 7

The creek that ran behind the house was swollen with rain water; John and Katherine were perched on rocks, their feet dangling in the water. Gabriel was on the far side of the creek, his fishing pole bobbing in the current. I searched everywhere for Becca but couldn't find her. I moved closer to Katherine so that I could hear their hushed conversation.

"When exactly are you leaving?"

"Tomorrow at first light." John leaned his head down on her shoulder and Katherine immediately scooted farther away and shot a look in Gabe's direction.

"John, we have to be careful."

"Stop being so worried all the time, Kat."

"I can't help it. Pa hasn't exactly given us his blessing."

"Would it help if I talked to him? Told him I plan to come back for you when you turn 18?"

"Oh, I don't know, he can be so unpredictable at times. I don't want to think about it. Right now, I just want to think about you leaving me."

John didn't care that Gabe was so close, he leaned over and kissed Katherine, the most endearing, heartfelt kiss; I felt it on my lips.

She gently pushed him away while the blush grew on her cheeks.

"How am I going to go on without you here?"

"Promise me something."

"Anything."

"When you wake up every day, I want you to think of my face, think of me kissing you good morning. Think of me telling you, "I love you". Then I want you to smile and go about your day, wrapped in the warmth that my love will give you. Don't be sad. Know that wherever I am, I am thinking about you, whenever you are thinking about me. One day we will be together forever. I give you my promise, Katherine Adkins."

Katherine leaned her head on his shoulder for just a minute and kissed him gently. "I promise."

"EWWWW Katherine, that's gross." Gabriel kicked at the water throwing a spray in their direction.

"Gabriel Adkins, if you say anything to anyone, I will make sure you regret it."

"Don't worry, I wouldn't wish Pa's wrath on anyone, not even you. My lips are sealed, as long as you do my barn chores for me this week."

Gabe flashed a huge smile and ran off in the direction of the house, his pole and bucket bouncing off his hip as he ran.

"I wish there were some way I could come over in the morning to see you off, but I know Pa would never let me."

"It's OK, Kat, I would rather say goodbye like this, just the two of us." A tear slid down his cheek, and Katherine gasped a bit before her tears started their own lonely trek.

John and Katherine sat on the rock, their hands squeezed together, their heads gently touching. The breeze from the trees whipped Katherine's hair around her face, and John inhaled her scent. Tears filled my eyes, blurring my vision and the scene before me.

I woke with the sinking feeling that John was gone. It saddened me almost as much as it did Katherine. My surly mood followed me through the morning. I wanted to finish the painting for James and Elise and take it to them tonight. It was the night I told Jack I would go to the bonfire with him, but something had to improve my mood or I knew I would have to back out somehow.

Something had changed when I thought of Jack. There was this shared connection that I felt grow even stronger, knowing that he was sharing the world of John and Katherine with me. It was almost as if he had stepped into my soul and was traveling the world with me. I knew that being with him would be different now, and as much as I wanted to fight it, I knew that I couldn't.

I still wasn't sure I liked it, how I really felt about it. As with many things in my life, I tried my best to avoid thinking about it, but spending time with Jack was not going to allow me to do that. Maybe I could get him to agree not to discuss it; it was doubtful, but worth a try.

The rain outside just soured my mood even more. It was hard to concentrate on the painting, and my tears blurred my vision as I tried to recreate the happy little cottage on the lake. Concentrating on making this a perfect gift for Elise and James was difficult but also helpful in putting the dreams out of my head. However, it was replaced with the knowledge that I would be leaving this place in a few weeks, and I wasn't ready to deal with that either. All of my life I had thought about my future and what I had to do to get there. I had always set goals for myself and then struggled to meet them. Now I wasn't sure what my goals were anymore. When my mom died, she took my future with her, and I still wasn't sure what it looked like anymore.

I finished the painting and decided to take it down to the market. I carefully placed the painting in a large garbage bag to protect it from the rain, secretly hoping that the rain would have cancelled the bonfire.

Elise and James went crazy over my painting; Elise cried when I gave it to her. There was a little argument about whether it should be hung in the market or in the house. They decided that it would start out in the market but they would move it to the house for the winter months. I watched as Jack and James hung it over the small table with the cash register. It looked like it was made for that spot.

The happiness that the painting brought to Elise and James completely turned my mood around and it also pushed the rain right out of the sky. So after we had dinner, Jack and I started out hand in hand for the bon fire. I didn't even mind that he had grabbed my hand. I told him as we walked that I was nervous about meeting his friends. He assured me that his friends were great and would be very welcoming.

Jack had apparently told them all about me because they treated me like a celebrity, which would have normally annoyed me if they weren't all so charming. His buddy, Alton, was tending to the fire as we settled down on the small patch of sand.

I was introduced to Billy and his girlfriend, Lainey, who was very plain and beautiful. Their English accents mesmerized me as we chatted about the lake and my visit. A tall, dark haired girl named Sabrina stuck very close to me and wanted to know all about America. Dax, a shy boy, hung close to Jack but seemed to only have eyes for Sabrina, although she seemed oblivious.

I wondered what Jack had told them about me. I watched Billy and Lainey kissing and holding hands, and a part of me longed for that, too.

At one point, Jack and Dax ran off down the beach a bit and were throwing a ball back and forth. I watched them lazily as Sabrina prattled on beside me about her favorite American actors, asking whether I had seen this movie or that TV show.

Alton had made the fire a bit too large, and the smoke and flames were all I could see. I couldn't see Jack and Dax anymore through the haze. I moved a bit further around the ring to try to get sight of them back. I didn't like Jack being that far away from me, even though I was becoming comfortable with this small group.

Billy began playing some tunes on his guitar, and the bottle of Jack Daniels was being passed around. No one seemed to care when I passed it up. Just as I passed the bottle to Sabrina, who took a long pull, I heard the splash.

I stood up to find out what was going on; the water at night was particularly scary to me. I caught sight of Jack swimming out into the lake to retrieve the ball. He only had the light of the half moon to lead his way. Fear grew from deep within, and I began to run down the sand, yelling his name.

When I reached Dax, I was out of breath and screaming Jack's name.

"Hey, hey Ava, he's fine. No one swims better than Jack." Dax threw his arm around my shoulders to reassure me.

I tried to focus my eyes on Jack out in the middle of the lake. He looked OK. He had retrieved the ball and was heading back toward shore. Part of me expected him to be pulled under by some invisible force. The terror inside me refused to leave until Jack was standing in front of me, shaking his head and spraying water all over me.

He grabbed me up in a bear hug and explained to Dax, "She doesn't like the water."

He then planted a kiss on my cheek and whispered in my ear, "Sorry I scared you."

This sent electricity through my body, forcing the terror out, replacing it with warmth that began spreading through me.

I didn't leave Jack's side the rest of the night. He took a few sips off the bottle of whiskey but stopped after he noticed that I wasn't drinking any. It was nice being wrapped in Jack's warmth, and for once I let myself enjoy it. The emotion of the past few days seeped out of me. At some point I think I started to doze on Jack's shoulder.

I could see the tiny, flickering flame of the lantern long before anything else came into view. I was drawn to it, seeing little else anyway. As more and more was revealed, I could make out Katherine, sitting on her bed, leaning over toward the lantern, reading a piece of paper, a smile and tears glistening on her face.

I wanted so desperately to read over her shoulder, but there was no room for me and I couldn't figure out how to maneuver around her. I watched as she reread at least five letters, sometimes with lines furrowing her brow. The one that made her smile she reread again and clutched the pages to her chest as she blew out the candle and lay down.

I waited until she was asleep and the letters had fallen out of her hand. Very carefully I leaned down and plucked one of the letters off of the quilt. Sitting down on the floor, I turned it over in my hands. John's handwriting was choppy, yet elegant. I began to read:

My dear Kat,

Today was a long day on the railroad, it is well after dark, and I am using a tiny lantern to write this letter to you as I don't know when I will have the time to again. Big Mike was happy with my work and has agreed to let me take some time off to go visit Ma. That along with the bonus I received will give me what

I need to come and get you! And your pa can't say anything about it because you are now 18.

Yes Katherine, this means I am coming for you and should be there by the next full moon; keep watching it, baby, it will bring me back to you. I think I am too excited to sleep but also know that I will pay for it tomorrow. So for now my sweet love, I am enclosing my heart in this letter for I know that you will take good care of it until we are together again.

All of my love,

Forever,

John

The tears were making tracks down my cheeks as I read the last lines. Just as Katherine had done earlier, I clutched it to my chest and watched Katherine's sleeping serene face. She would get to be with her John. This warmed my heart. As the minutes clicked by, something itched at the back of my brain. Something didn't feel right.

My eyes furrowed; I replaced the letter and stood over Katherine, wondering what was going on in her dreams. This unsettling feeling began to quiver and I had to step away from the bed, grabbing at the small dresser to regain myself.

I startled when I heard a voice close by, "Come on bug, it's time to go."

John was here; that's what he called Becca. I turned to find him and immediately lost sight of everything, as if it had been sucked away.

"Come on bug, it's time to go." Jack's voice sounded in my ear, soft and breathy.

He called me "bug". It itched at the back of my brain, but the fogginess of sleep and the exertion of standing to my feet forced it away almost instantly.

We walked back to his house, hand in hand. We were both quiet, lost in thought. I wasn't fully awake to be having coherent thoughts, except one that took hold: how was I going to leave here?

We were both too exhausted to say much when we got back to his house. Elise had already made up the couch for me. Jack disappeared for a few minutes and came back with a pillow and blanket. He threw them on the other couch and climbed in under the blanket. Then his eyes met mine.

We stared at each other for a long time, our thoughts reaching out in a million different directions. Still neither of us spoke. When I was under my blanket, he came over to me slowly and bent down so that his face was right in front of mine. I could smell his breath, warm on my face.

His lips reached out to mine.

I didn't know if I was dreaming, but the sensations that shot from my lips to my toes made me blush. He stopped long before I was ready for him to, and when I opened my eyes, he was already back under his blanket. The last thing I heard from across the room, muffled by the blankets was "Thank you."

"Katherine. Katherine!" I could hear Becca calling for her before I saw her. "Please let me put my feet in. It's so hot out."

Becca and Katherine were sitting on the bank of the creek, swollen from heavy rains. The dew and raindrops lay heavy all around. Katherine was lost in her thoughts, a pile of papers clutched to her chest. She wasn't paying any attention to Becca, who was inching closer and closer to the water's edge.

I started to run around the bank, ready to go in after Becca if I needed to. The creek wasn't wide, but it looked to be deep in the center and all around were rocks of varying sizes. It looked like someone stood on the bank and threw these gigantic rocks into the creek bed and where they landed was where they stayed.

Becca was prattling on about something or other, and Katherine was now reading one of John's letter's, I assumed. It all seemed to happen in a blink; one minute Becca was on the bank and the next she was in the center of the creek, its rushing waters overtaking her. I stood frozen. I wouldn't be able to grab her. Katherine was still lost in her letters and I reached out and smacked the letter out of her hand. It worked. The letter tumbled onto the grass just as Becca's first scream reached Katherine's ears.

The terror in Katherine's face masked mine. We both ran to the edge of the creek. Katherine hiked her skirt up, grabbed at a long stick nearby, and walked out with as much urgency as she would allow over the rocks. She kept extending the stick out to gauge how much farther she would have to go. Their screams to each other echoed around the valley but also brought help. Pa came running with Gabriel at his heels, yelling for Katherine and Becca.

Pa pushed past Katherine and sloshed through the water to reach Becca. It was about chest high, and Pa had to maneuver around the rocks carefully. The water was rushing so fast past him that he had to grab on each rock to keep himself from being swept away. Becca had clung to one of the large rocks but appeared to be slipping under. Katherine was screaming and flailing all over the rock; it appeared as if she, too, was going to fall in.

He had reached Becca just in time to scoop her up in his arms while struggling to keep his footing. Very carefully but with as much urgency as he could, he maneuvered around the rocks back to the side.

Pa hoisted Becca up onto the mossy ground. Out of breath and spewing water on the ground, Pa fell to his knees, his hands on the ground next to Becca's head. Katherine fell at Becca's side and they both cried out to each other. I could feel every emotion Katherine felt, my chest heaving in great sobs that matched hers, my terror for Becca just as real.

I fell to my knees beside her. Katherine and Pa were yelling at her, at Gabriel to go get Ma, at each other, at no one in particular. In the midst of the chaos, Becca stilled and turned her eyes to me. She reached her hand out, but the exhaustion made it fall right back to the ground. I tried to grab her hand but couldn't grasp it. She closed her eyelids for a minute and began to sing her song as her breathing started to return to normal.

Sing to me softly

Sing to me clear

Birds in the treetop

Little Bird near

I woke with the last line of the song playing in my head, wiping away my tears. With each wipe, light filtered in through my eyelids.

Sing to me softly

Sing away my fear

In an instant I realized the dream was gone. I opened my eyes and was staring at the Hollings' brown leather couch back. The pillow beneath my head was wet. I sniffled and rolled over; my head, a bag of rocks, was too heavy to move. Jack's eyes were open and staring at me, just as they were the previous night.

"You were crying in your dream," he stated.

I sat up on the couch and sorted through the foggy memory. "Becca almost drowned in the creek."

"I know."

"What? You knew Becca almost drowned, and you didn't tell me?"

"Now wait a minute, Ava, that's not fair. I just dreamt about it that day when you and Mum were cooking. I didn't know then that this was all…real? I don't know, I guess I didn't put it all together after I found out."

I hung my head, knowing he was right.

"I'm sorry, you're right. I think this is getting to be a little too much for me. When I first started dreaming about them, it was sweet, but now…I don't know, it's just…strange."

I half laughed as the realization of these dreams was sinking in. I sat up on the couch taking huge breaths to try to clear my head, erase the dream and all the emotions that came with it.

Not wanting to think about it anymore, I folded the blankets and cleaned up the couch while Jack made us some breakfast. Neither one of us spoke for quite awhile. Both of us were lost in thought, and I was struggling with making sense of everything that had happened over the past few days: my feelings for Jack, leaving this place I had grown to love, the crazy dreams, all of it.

After breakfast was cleaned up, I sat back down on the couch, exhausted already. Jack joined me, sitting a little too close for my comfort. When he started to speak, I stopped him.

"I don't want to think about the dreams too much, to give them too much attention, because I don't want to have to admit that they might have been real."

Jack bit his lower lip and looked towards the kitchen as he mumbled. "Is that what you are doing with your feelings about me?"

"What, what do you, wait, you think…Jack…?"

Why was I getting defensive? I knew he was right but was having trouble admitting it. I put my head in my hands as the realization sunk in. This is what I had been doing with my feelings for Jack.

"I'm leaving, Jack, going back to North Carolina and my life. I don't know what to think."

Jack came to sit next to me and wrapped his hands in mine. We sat in silence, neither one knowing what to say.

"I have a life waiting for me in North Carolina, Jack."

This was all I could say. I watched him hang his head as he squeezed his arms tighter around me. I shrugged out of them, feeling exhausted and fed up with all of it, the strange twist of my dreams, the change in my relationship with Jack that I was not ready to accept. It was all too much for my mind to handle.

"What's wrong?"

"I don't know, Jack. I don't know anything anymore. These dreams are starting to freak me out, and I just wish they would stop."

"How can you say that?"

"What do you mean how can I say that? I am done with them. I am tired of waking up wrapped in the emotions of some stupid people that keep showing up in my dreams. I don't need their problems added to mine. Maybe going back to North Carolina is just what I need."

"Ava, they are not just some dream people. It means something. At least to me it does."

Jack pushed himself farther away from me and hung his head. I knew exactly what he was saying, and I didn't like it. Jack wanted to put some romantic spin on all of this, and I certainly wasn't ready to hear anything about it.

"Jack, why do you insist on being so pigheaded?"

"I'm not being pigheaded, I'm stating a fact. Katherine and John were us."

"That is nonsense, craziness. They are people in a dream, something our minds have fabricated. They were not real people, and they were certainly not us. When you first said that, I thought it was kind of cute, but now I just think it is all nonsense."

"You have been dreaming of Katherine since you got here. I have been dreaming about John for years. Explain to me how we both ended up in the same dream?"

"I can't explain it. And that is just your opinion, Jack, it doesn't mean we are meant for each other." I rolled my eyes trying to make my point more than obvious.

"Ava, I know this might sound strange, but I have had years to think about these dreams. I know that I was John, in some other life. Like reincarnation. I think that we live multiple lives, learning things along the way, until we get it right. I have learned so much from John, he helps me to figure life out, you know? Like the way you are afraid of the water. Becca almost drowned, and in some deep part of your soul, a part that lived many, many years ago, you remember what it felt like to almost lose her. It explains why you are afraid of the water."

"That's absurd, Jack! I don't understand the dreams at all, and I am not sure I want to learn anything from them. I am afraid of the water because I never learned to swim, period." I hung my head, a bit ashamed. "I can't explain it Jack, I just…I don't know anymore what I think."

Jack moved closer to me on the couch and gently turned my shoulders so that I was looking right at him.

"Then explain this."

He leaned in and kissed me. I tried to fight him, but my lips had another idea. They felt like they finally had a purpose, as if they now knew their reason for being. The pit of my stomach dropped, and my arms went numb. How could this be so right, yet so very wrong? I wanted to push him away, but the more his lips caressed mine, the more my body said, "Don't stop." His tongue gently forced my lips open, and fire shot though my head. His breathe engulfed mine and tasted like every wonderful thing I had ever tasted. I didn't want him to stop.

Slowly my fingers found his hair and lost themselves in the silky mess. I had never felt more at home in my entire life. Slowly he pulled away, and our eyes were lost in each other for the longest time. Finally I spoke, but my words were not what my body was screaming. I could hear myself speaking as if I were in another room.

"Jack, I can't, I have to leave in two weeks. I can't fall in love with you."

"Too late, Missy." He kissed my nose.

"Stop!" I yelled. "This is not going to happen. I have…"

"Plans, yeah I know, it's all I've bloody heard about all summer."

Jack grabbed my hand and pressed his lips to them, sending my mind spiraling back to John doing the same thing to Katherine. I pushed against his legs so that there was a little more space between us.

"I need some time to think."

Jack looked at me like I had smacked him in the face.

"What is there to think about? We have found each other. Do you know how rare this is? Life has brought us together again, and I am not willing to let you go again."

"Jack, you say this like you remember. The only reason you think you remember is because of the dreams. They didn't really happen. It wasn't us."

"How do you know?" he asked. His voice rising, the anger clear on his face.

"I don't know, but everything that I do know tells me that there is no way this is real. I'm sorry, I know you feel differently." I stood up off the couch and gathered my things to leave. "Please, Jack, please let me go and think."

"Ava, I love you, and I know that makes you uncomfortable, but by that kiss we just had, I know you love me, too, you just can't admit it." He stood up and kissed my forehead and added, "This is us."

My mind couldn't take anymore; it was as if I were two parts of a spinning top, each part going in the opposite direction. I ran out of his house and down the road home. I craved the separation, the time alone to think. The tears were streaming now, and I wished that my mom were here to comfort me and help me make sense of everything.

When I got to the top of the lane leading to the cottage, the tears were nearly blinding me. My legs sent me running down the lane toward the safety of the cottage, but my mind was jumbling all over the place. My feet were moving a little too fast and caught on a tree root about halfway down the path. I tumbled forward, the ground racing up to meet my face. I felt my legs buckle under me and heard the crack at the same time my head bounced off another tree root. I rolled a few feet and slammed into the base of a large oak.

I couldn't catch my breath; the searing pain in my arm overtook the throbbing of my head. I couldn't move. I think I lost consciousness for a few moments and was barely aware of the thick red blood dribbling down my head into my eyes. I don't know how long I lay like that with the pain forcing me in and out of awareness. The sounds of birds singing in the trees overhead wove their way into my thoughts, and Becca's song was bouncing off the inside of my brain.

Birds in the branches

Sing songs from above.

High in the heavens

Sing a song of love.

Birds in the treetops

Little bird near

Sing to me softly

Sing away my fear.

I needed help. Moving very slowly, I reached a few feet away to grab my backpack and my phone with my good arm, the pain shooting again through my left arm. I had to wipe the blood from my eyes with my sleeve to dial Jack's number. He answered on the first ring.

"Yo babe, can't stay mad at me long, huh?"

"Jack, I need help. I've fallen. I think I broke something." I could only get that out as the pain in my arm almost caused the world to leave again.

"Ava, where are you?"

"I'm in front of the cottage."

"On my way, stay on the phone with me."

"Hurry." That was all I could get out before the phone dropped from my hands to the moss below.

I could hear Jack yelling through the phone, panic making his voice rise every time he called my name. I don't know how long I lay there, but what seemed like an eternity passed, and I began to hear Jack's screams now through the trees and echoing in the phone by my ear.

He reached me and fell to his knees, dropping his phone within inches of mine.

"Oh Ava, your arm." He dropped his backpack on the ground and grabbed a towel from inside and gently began dabbing at my head.

"I'm going to have to call for an ambulance, you need to go to the A&E."

"NO, please no, just help me up and inside."

"Ava, your arm is definitely broken; you won't be able to get up. SHHH, it will be OK; let me call Mum."

I gave up protesting, giving in to the pain shooting up my arm mixing with the throbbing of my forehead.

Elise and James came with the car. Just seeing Elise's calm face brought me a bit of peace. Jack couldn't hide the terror on his face, and James walked him a few feet away with his arm around him so that he could collect himself. I knew he was feeling guilty. I searched Elise's face which reassured me that everything was going to be OK.

Elise and James braced me as best they could, and with enough pain to knock me out a few more times, I was loaded in the back of their car.

Jack never left my side in the A&E, which I came to find out stands for Accident and Emergency. He was able to compose himself enough to hold my hand through the seven stitches to my forehead and the intensity of positioning and casting my arm. My eyes never left Jack's except when I had to clench them shut to scream in pain. In my quest to force the pain out of my body, I squeezed both of his hands with my good hand, but he never complained.

It was hours and many pain pills later that I was able to formulate sentences. I was lying on the Hollings' couch with my cast propped up on two pillows. Elise and James insisted that I stay with them, and I was so grateful. Jack waited on my every need. Slowly, his playful side took back over, and he eventually had me laughing though the pain.

"You can sure be a real pain in the...errr... arm, Ava." Jack busted out laughing, his head thrown back like a little child. My lips curved up in a smile; he was the pain sometimes.

"You're the pain in the...arm, Jack."

"Oh Ava, you've got me in stitches over here." And again the laughter filled the room. How could I stay mad at him?

When I was trying to adjust myself to a sitting position on the couch, Jack added, "Don't break a bone over there, Miss Banks," to which I responded with a throw pillow in his face.

I made the call to Aunt Cathy late that night. She wanted to hop on the next plane, but I assured her I was fine. She talked to Elise for a long time and was finally convinced that I was in good hands. I fell asleep listening to Elise's reassuring comments to her on the phone and Jack's soft snoring on the couch next to me.

Chapter 8

I could feel Jack's hand entwined in mine long before I realized where I was. The surroundings were very unfamiliar to me, and there was a haze all around me that made it difficult to make out exactly what was in front of me. I squeezed Jack's hand tighter, and he whispered to me, "Shhh, it's OK."

I could tell he had been here before as he gently pulled me forward. The scene began to take shape. We were in a small tent it seemed. Thick cigar smoke threatened to choke us and stung my eyes. We moved closer to a figure hunched over on a cot. It was John. I looked at Jack quizzically, and he squeezed my hand reassuringly. On the cot next to John was another man huddled under blankets, even though it appeared to be midsummer.

"I don't care what he said, you are not leaving."

"You are not my superior, and I will leave when I am good and ready." John straightened his back a bit as the other man grumbled to himself.

"Not if I have anything to do with it, you're not. You can't just abandon us out here to finish up this damned railroad. You came here to do a job."

"I have done my work and done it well, and if Big Mike doesn't have a problem with me leaving for a few weeks then I think you should just mind your own business. I have family to tend to, not that it should matter to you."

Before John could get the last word out, the other man was off his cot and caught John in the jaw before he could ever react. John hit the floor with a thud.

Jack dropped my hand and ran to him, crouching by his side. It almost appeared as if John looked right up into Jack's eyes as he forced himself up off the floor to confront the man. I could see John straighten his back as he shook his head and caressed his jaw.

The man stood in front of John, provoking him with his fists raised. John shook his head again and banged out the door mumbling behind him, "Not worth it."

Jack and I followed him out the door and across the green grass to another tent. No one was inside, and John slumped down on the cot, his head in his hands. Jack immediately went right over to him and sat down next to him. I stood and watched the two men share a moment of silence. It was amazing to me to see them side by side. They looked so different in appearance but shared the same pained expression. John began to mumble to himself.

"I hate it here. I can't take it anymore. Oh my dear Katherine, how long do I have to wait to be by your side forever? I miss everything about you." *He looked up and stared in my directions and continued,* *"It's almost as if I can smell you, feel you with me. I have to get out of this God forsaken place."* *His tears began to slide down his face, and I watched Jack put his hand over top of John's as if he were giving him strength. John scratched his hand just where Jack's hand rested. He was lost in thought and heaved a giant sigh as he wiped his face of the tears, trying to regain his composure.*

I just stood in place, watching Jack comfort John and take away his pain, it seemed. Jack looked up at me and smiled reassuringly. I walked over to him and gently ran my fingers through his hair.

"Ava, it's time for you to eat something so you can take your next pain pill."

My eyes snapped open, dissolving the scene before me. Adjusting my eyes, I could just make out Elise standing over me holding a bowl of something steaming. I looked around, startled, until I remembered where I was. I winced in pain as I tried to maneuver myself so that I was sitting up and could accept the bowl.

Jack stirred next to me on the other couch. He sat up rubbing his eyes. "Geesh Mum, why did you have to wake us up?"

"I'm sorry dear, but Ava has to eat or the medicine will upset her stomach, and if she doesn't take another pain pill soon, the pain would have woken her up."

I gratefully accepted the bowl of soup and arranged it on the tray that James had fashioned for me. It was difficult to balance the bowl and eat with one arm, but I refused any help and vowed to figure that part out on my own.

Jack was in a bad mood as he often was when he just woke up. It took him a few minutes to gather himself together and sit up on the couch. Once Elise retreated to the kitchen, Jack inched closer to me on the couch.

"I always hate when I have to comfort John; it seems to take so much out of me."

I just stared at him, not knowing what to say. I still wasn't comfortable sharing these dreams with him, and it always took me by surprise when he so nonchalantly discussed them. He had an obvious bond with John that I was not ready to accept. He had been living with them longer than I had, and until just a few days ago, they had been mine and mine alone.

I tried to change the subject whenever he brought it up or when we shared a dream. I didn't like talking about them, and it was still hard enough being a part of them while I was sleeping. I also did not want to have the same argument with him over and over again.

Over the next few days, as I was convalescing at their house, the dreams had taken on a new quality. Jack and I were often together now in the dreams as he slept in the den with me on a regular basis. When I did nap, while he was busy working or taking some rare time away, they were always sad dreams of Katherine missing John or John missing Katherine. It was heart wrenching to watch, and I was beginning to understand what Jack meant by draining.

It seemed as if every emotion that I had was spent in my dreams. Sometimes the dreams were of happy times when Katherine, Becca, and Gabriel were younger. There was no particular order to the dreams, which made it very difficult to handle sometimes. Often dreams would skip around in order, depicting Katherine's life as a child and her and John's love in the same night.

I had a particularly disturbing dream one day while Jack was with the campers.

The field was low as if the wheat hadn't been planted for long. Gabriel and Pa were crouched low at the far end of the field. It didn't take me long to reach them. Gabe looked to be in a particularly surly mood and Pa had a faraway look in his eyes as if he wasn't entirely all there.

"Pa, why do we plant and harvest wheat?"

"Git to work boy, this isn't time for blabbering."

"I was just wondering why we didn't plant something else is all."

Pa's backhand found Gabe's mouth with ease, knocking him off his feet.

"What did I say about your mouth? Git back to work, and don't open that mouth again. What we plant is my business, not yours."

Gabe was trying to be a man and not cry; he puffed up his shoulders, and for a minute I thought he was going to charge Pa. His shoulders hunched just as quickly, the look of defeat all over his face.

I watched the two of them for some time, silently working in the new wheat fields. I wanted to reach out and touch Gabe, let him know that it was all going to be OK. But I wasn't sure that it would be. Something inside told me that it wouldn't be.

I wanted to leave this dream, the anguish was too much, and I looked around for a way out. I pleaded with myself and tried to wake up, but I couldn't. I felt trapped and almost as if I couldn't breathe. I turned and ran back through the fields, desperate to leave this scene.

I tripped and fell a few times but kept propelling myself forward, willing myself to wake up. The harder I tried to free myself from the dream, the more vivid it became. I could see the house in the distance and kept moving in that direction.

The house was unfamiliar, the roof strangely angled. It was facing in the wrong direction. I tried to stop my feet from running when I realized that I was going in the wrong direction. This wasn't the home I knew. The more I tried to stop, the faster I ran. I had no control in this dream, couldn't stop it or stop myself from racing forward.

Finally I skidded to a stop in front of a small framed house, smoke billowing out of the chimney. The smell of cinnamon stopped me in my tracks. Shaking my head to try to dispel the smell, I had no idea where I was. My confused mind searched the surroundings for something familiar. Panic started to rise in my chest. The dreams had always been familiar to me, as if I knew my way around them. This scene was different, yet somewhere deep in the recesses of my mind I knew it was not completely unfamiliar, but I couldn't conjure up what I knew about it.

I plopped down on the soft ground, trying to figure it all out. That is when he emerged from the house. I watched him walk into the barn, his head bent low. It was Peter, John's dad.

I scrambled to my feet, following closely behind him. The need for information about him thrust me forward. When I reached the barn, I could see that Peter had joined Albert at the far end. I scrambled through the propped open door and gingerly walked within inches of the men.

Pa appeared to be much younger than he had in the field moments earlier. His face was eager and happy, jovial even. It didn't fit with the man I had come to know.

"Peter, my man, are you ready for this?"

"Albert, I hope you know what you are doing."

"Wheat is the answer my friend. We will soon be providing for our families like never before. Peter, my pal, we will be the talk of the valley. Every family will want to trade with us for our wheat. Trust me. I know exactly what I am doing."

Peter pounded Albert on his back, the smile growing across his face. The two men got to work harnessing the team as if they were one. The friendship, the teamwork, and the camaraderie were palpable.

I wanted to smile but knew too much to allow any happiness to invade this scene. If anything, it made me sad. The sadness served as a force to push me awake.

My body jerked, sending a wave of pain down my arm, which had somehow been pinned under my body on the couch. Gingerly, I moved my body so that I was sitting up.

"You OK, sweetie?" Elise's voice came softly from the kitchen.

"Yeah, I think so; my arm is just throbbing a bit."

"You were thrashing around a bit in your sleep. Here, let me get you some pills to help with the pain."

"No, no that is OK. I don't like those pills much." I wanted to stay away from anything that would force me back to sleep. I was starting to resent the dreams. "It will pass I just have to keep it elevated for a bit." I propped my cast up on a few pillows and forced a smile in Elise's direction.

"Rudyard Kipling wrote, 'If you can dream, and not make dreams your master.' Dreams can be a very powerful thing, Ava. Take from them what you need to, but don't be a slave to them." Elise set an ice cold tea on my tray and headed back to the kitchen. I stared at her for a long time, trying to make sense of what she had just said. How did she know? What did it mean? My dreams, my whole life had changed this year so dramatically with the loss of my mom. My life was no longer what I had dreamed it to be, and I was trying so hard to hold on to it. Maybe Elise was right, I shouldn't make them my master.

So what of the nighttime dreams I was having, were they controlling me now, too? It certainly felt as if I were giving too much power to these dreams but had no power myself to stop them.

"Elise, what poem is that from?"

She scurried to her old cupboard and retrieved a battered old book. She flipped through the pages trying to find the poem.

"Here it is. 'IF' by Rudyard Kipling. You know this lake is named after him."

"Yes, Jack told me. Thanks, I'd like to read it."

Elise left me with the book. I read the poem over and over again, and each time I took from it something new and different. It felt like it was speaking to me in some ways but speaking of Jack in others.

> *If you can keep your head when all about you*
> *Are losing theirs and blaming it on you;*
> *If you can trust yourself when all men doubt you,*
> *But make allowance for their doubting too:*
> *If you can wait and not be tired by waiting,*

I kept reading this over and over again, thinking about Jack and how easily he traveled through life, rarely getting angry, especially at me, who he had every reason to be angry with lately. He stood so firmly on his belief that these dreams had been real, and I had to give him some credit for that.

When Jack came home, he saw the book sitting next to me on the couch opened to the poem and started chuckling.

"If you can meet with Triumph and Disaster and treat those two impostors just the same," he recited from memory. "My favorite line." He plopped down on the couch next to me and laid his head on my shoulder. "Missed you today."

I sighed and tilted my head to meet his. I was tired and full of emotion from trying to make sense of everything around me.

I decided not to tell Jack about the dreams. Even so, Jack seemed to know that something was wrong by my melancholy.

"What's wrong, seen a ghost?"

"Well, I sorta have."

Jack nodded as if he understood. He shifted around on the couch next to me and searched my eyes for answers.

"I really don't feel like it, Jack."

"Sometimes talking about it helps."

"I'm tired of talking about it. It seems like that is all we do anymore, and it is exhausting. Isn't there anything else we can talk about? Something real?"

Jack sat back, a little dejected, and heaved a sigh. He looked at me with sadness in his eyes. While he was enlivened by these dreams, I was just depleted.

"And so hold on when there is nothing in you except the will which says to them: 'Hold on!'" Jack whispered in my ear, and I recognized the words from the poem. It seemed like all I had been doing since my mom died was holding on.

I heard a knock at the door and watched Elise let in Dax and Sabrina. I was happy to see them and put some distance between me, Jack, and the dreams.

Jack and Dax went out to the boat, leaving me to share all the details of my accident with Sabrina, so happy for the diversion. She wanted to know every detail, but I chose to give her the abridged version.

She had given me a book to read and was embarrassed when she realized that she forgot to take the price tag off of it: £11.17. I gasped when I saw it but quickly hid my surprise not wanting to tell Sabrina about this strange number which was still following me. I was grateful when she finally focused on herself.

"So Dax finally asked me out." She said as she sat on the ground next to me. "I've been waiting forever, and after the bonfire the other night, he walked me home, and we've been together ever since. I mean, we've been friends for years, and finally I think he's noticed me, like really noticed me."

"That's great; he seems like one of the good guys."
"So what's up with you and Jack? I know, I'm not

supposed to ask, he told us not to discuss it with you, but come on, he's a dream."

This made me laugh and blush a little.

"Jack and I are good friends. I am leaving in two weeks to go home, and I don't want to even think about leaving him as it is. So just friends."

"Well, I think you should, you know, go for it. You can't tell me you don't see how he feels about you. I have known him almost all my life, and I have never seen him look at a girl the way he looks at you."

I put my head down, not wanting to hear this, but knowing it was true. I liked Sabrina and felt that maybe I could talk to her.

"I don't know, it's just something I promised myself, that I wouldn't have any commitments when I left here. I came here to paint and grieve for my mother and suddenly found this amazing family and person that now I can't imagine not having in my life."

I stopped and thought for a minute and then continued, "Long distance relationships never work, but I know we will remain friends forever."

"You and I both can see that it is more than friendship to him."

I couldn't answer her, so I just stared at the floor, letting her words linger in my head.

Sabrina babbled on and on, and I just watched her lips, trying to make sense of what she was saying. My thoughts went to home and what was waiting for me there. I would have to tell Aunt Cathy and Uncle Bern that I wasn't going to Stanford. I was so nervous how they would react. I had already done a little research on the local community colleges and figured that I would start a semester there and then transfer to a four year college.

"All I know is that you and Jack are perfect together. He had a girlfriend last year. Did he tell you about her?"

I'm not sure what I had missed from Sabrina, but her question startled me.

"No, he only said that he had had a girlfriend but then didn't offer anything else about it, and I didn't ask."

"It was a mess; he was such a good boyfriend, as I am sure you can imagine, and she was just awful to him. We all hated her, yet he was too caught up in having a girlfriend to see what was right in front of his face: a two faced cheater who just broke his heart."

"The land of denial is wide and deep, my friend."

Was I living in my own land of denial? But what was I in denial about? Is that part of denial, too?

"Well, we all think you and Jack are perfect together." Sabrina gave me a hug and then signed my cast just as Dax and Jack bounded back in the door.

I watched as the three of them played a game of Wii Tennis. I kept catching Jack's eyes on me and was powerless to look away. He winked, and it sent a chill down my spine. I had to take a long drink of my soda and look away to regain myself.

"So the boat should be ready for sailing by the weekend. Who is in for a boat tour of the lake?" Jack looked at me tentatively.

"I am not going anywhere out on that water, and you know it." I stared down at my cast, although I knew he wouldn't let that keep me from getting on the stupid boat. Jack waited until Dax and Sabrina left to bring it up again.

Cuddled on his couch, his hand casually on my leg, the other draped over the back of the couch, he began.

"I know you have a fear of the water, and now we know why, but I think we need to confront that fear and get you out there. I promise you nothing will happen to you; I will be right there beside you the whole time. You can even wear a life jacket, and we will stay close to the shore."

"Why are you so intent on getting me out there?"

"Because it is a part of me, and I want to share it with you, and I know that you would love it, once you allow yourself to get past the fear of it."

"Right now I have more important things to worry about than going out on that silly boat."

I held up my casted arm and winced a bit from lingering pain.

"And I have to tell Aunt Cathy and Uncle Bern that I am not going to Stanford. I was going to tell them when they came, but now, I don't know, I have to tell them soon. They will be expecting me to be home by August 1st and then ready to go to school by the 15th. I have deceived them long enough, and I am not sure they will be too happy with me."

"I understand."

He rubbed my back and kissed my head. I pulled my head away from his kiss and shot him a look, which I know upset him.

"Can you do me a favor? I need my laptop from the cottage so I can Skype them and let them know. I better get it over with."

"Sure thing." He bounded off the couch, grateful, I guess, for the distraction. I know I was.

I decided that the best approach would be to just be honest. I owed so much to them and didn't want to disappoint them. Aunt Cathy was my mom's best friend since grade school. When she got pregnant with me, we moved into their house and lived there until I was 5, and my mom finished school and became a school nurse. My mom and I then moved just around the corner from them, and they had always been second parents to me. Aunt Cathy was not able to get pregnant, so I became like a daughter to them. When mom died, it was only natural for them to continue to look after me.

Uncle Bern was an engineer and had also inherited money when his father died. Aunt Cathy and Uncle Bern always lived well, and I had always wondered if the only reason my mom and I were able to live as we did was because of them.

When Jack returned with my laptop, I set up the webcam and rang them through Skype. It didn't take them long to answer; I am sure they were expecting my call.

"Hey darling, you are looking good. How is the arm?" Uncle Bern said.

"It's OK, just a pain, literally. Elise, James, and Jack have been great, taking really good care of me. Where is Aunt Cathy?"

"She isn't back from book club yet. I expected her by now. Please thank the Hollings for us. I am so glad that you have them."

"I will. I wish you could meet them. Maybe one day you will. Well, I am sort of glad Cathy isn't there; I need to talk to you, and it might be better to tell you first."

"Is everything OK?"

"Um, yeah, well you see, after Mom died, everything was such a blur, and in that blur, I forgot to mail back my acceptance letter to Stanford." I bit my lip waiting for his reply.

"OK, hmm, well I can certainly understand how that happened. I can always call the dean and see if there is anything that we can do? Maybe you can start in January?"

"You're not mad?"

"No sweetheart, this is your life, and we are here to help you in any way that we can, but you are an adult now and need to make these decisions for yourself. Cathy and I will always be here to support you in whatever way you need us."

I wanted to reach through the phone and hug him. He was always unpredictable; I guess I caught him on a good day?

"Well, how do you think Aunt Cathy is going to take it?"

"Don't worry about her. I will smooth things over with her. Now how about letting me call the dean?"

"NO really, no, that is OK. I can take this semester off or go to community college for a year."

We said our goodbyes, and I slumped to the floor, hugging my knees with my good arm. A slow, wide smile spread across my radiant face. My love for Uncle Bern warmed my heart, and I knew that everything would be OK. I missed him and Aunt Cathy so much, and I finally had hope that maybe things would be alright when I got home. This got me thinking about going back to the cottage, finishing my paintings and starting to put the finishing touches on my summer in England as well.

I was tired of being emotional and wrapped up in these dreams that just seemed to exhaust me. Jack obviously thought about them in a different way than I did, and I wasn't sure I could handle too much more of either of them.

Elise and James were not happy about my decision to go back to the cottage.

"Honey, you are welcome to stay here until you go back to the states. We love having you here."

"That is very kind, but I have so much I need to do at the cottage before I leave, and my days are dwindling. You and James have been so wonderful, and I will never forget it or you all."

"Well, we are not going anywhere, dear. We certainly think of you as family now."

"I know, me too. It is just going to be so hard to leave, and I think I should start that process now."

I took a long time packing up my things and getting back to the cottage. It wasn't that I wanted to leave, Elise had taken care of me so well and I was really comfortable there, but I knew it was for the best.

Jack walked me home and hung around while I put things away. Getting used to working with one arm was taking its toll on me, and I took it out on him.

"I am not an invalid, Jack," I snapped as he tried to help me plug in the laptop.

"Sorry, I was just trying to help. Are you sure you will be OK here tonight? I could stay?"

"Really Jack, I will be fine. Maybe it's best if you go back home, and I will call you if I need you."

The sad look on Jack's face stopped me in my tracks. I kept hurting him, and I didn't want to do that but wasn't sure how to stop. Too much had happened too quickly, and I couldn't figure out how to go forward.

"I'm sorry, Jack, I am just tired and need to start getting ready to go home. I leave in seven days, and I have so much to do."

"Let me help you. You never let me help. One of the things that I love about you is your strength and independence, but it is also one of the things about you that drives me crazy."

"Well, that is who I am, Jack. I am sorry if it hurts your feelings."

"I wish you would let me in."

"I am not having this argument with you again, Jack. Please don't make me say it over and over again."

We sat in silence for a few minutes. Jack moved a little closer to me and grabbed my hands. He lifted them to his mouth and kissed them softly. Neither one of us knew what to say. It had all been said already. Slowly he moved in to hug me, and I let him, relieved for a minute that his arms were around me. I couldn't fight it any longer. His hug was tight and comforting, and we stayed like that for a long time, my head resting on his shoulder. I don't know how long it was, but I opened my eyes when he kissed my forehead, and we broke apart very slowly.

Because neither one of us wanted to hurt the other any further, Jack reluctantly left. I watched him slowly meander up the path to the lane, his head hung low. Jack Hollings always seemed to make me smile, even when I was mad at him. I tried so hard to stuff away my feelings for him, but my heart couldn't help but smile because I knew I was a better person for having met him and his family; it was so bittersweet.

Chapter 9

I woke with the sun streaming in the bedroom window, beckoning me to greet the day. I didn't remember dreaming and felt more rested than I had in a long time. After I got dressed, I decided to take my coffee down to the train station; it had been so long since I had been on the train, and I wasn't sure I would have another opportunity to before I left. This made me sad, but that sadness was pushed aside by the bright, sunny day.

I arrived a little early and settled down on the bench to watch and wait. Edwards and Edwards were busy getting the train ready and didn't notice my arrival. They were arguing over something, which wasn't unusual, and I struggled to hear what they were saying.

"I just don't get all the excitement over it. It's a silly thing, really." Edwards was bent over, removing the block from behind the back wheels of the train.

"You always take away all the fun. Why can't you see how brilliant it is? And that it only happens once a year, that is just amazing."

"Well, I don't get it. A rock gets in the way, that is all it really is; like a tree or a cloud, it's no different."

"You have always been too levelheaded; you take the fun out of everything." Edwards passed by his brother and playfully punched him in the arm.

"You are a dreamer, my brother, always have been, always will be. You think everything has a meaning behind it, everything happens for a reason."

"And it does. The sun setting twice in one night makes me believe that we sometimes get a do over. Like when you fell off the wagon and then came here to work with me- you got a second chance."

"OK, Edwards, whatever you want to believe. I only came here to work with you because you can't survive without me. Damn train station went to hell while I was gone."

The way the brothers bantered back and forth made me smile. They were talking about the double sunset, the one I missed because I was too afraid to go out on the water. I didn't have time to ponder this because Edwards finally noticed me sitting on the bench, wrapped in my own amusement.

"Well look who it is, Miss America. Hey Edwards, she's back. See, I told you she wouldn't have gone home without saying goodbye. See, second chances." This sent Edwards into a fit of laughter. "What happened to your arm, Miss America?"

"Oh, stupid accident, apparently when you fall into a tree, the tree is harder than your arm." I shrugged and smiled to let him know I was alright. "But I am leaving in a few days, and I am going to miss my train rides."

"Hey Edwards, she is going to miss us, did you hear that? Let's give her a nice one today!"

He ushered me to my front seat, and even though the train was barely full, he blasted the whistle and the train began to lurch forward. The train whistle settled me in ways I will never understand.

The sun was bright and peeking its way through the trees as we slowly made our way out toward the lake. It made me think about what Edwards had said about second chances. Was this my second chance? My life certainly seemed to stop when my mom died. Nothing seemed to fit anymore into the puzzle pieces that I had laid out for my life long ago. Maybe it was time for me to begin a new puzzle, a new life, a new start. Something deep inside me was stirring with the possibilities. I watched the sun dart in and out of the trees and became hypnotized with the prospects before me.

When the train lurched back into the station, I felt dizzy. My mind was not used to thinking this way. I hugged Edwards and Edwards, feeling a bit uncharacteristically enthusiastic, and bounded back up the lane toward the cottage.

To calm my mind I knew there was only one thing I could do. I arranged my paints so that I could make the best use of my one good arm. It was difficult, but I managed. As I painted I thought about all of the changes that had happened in my life since coming to Rudyard Lake: The Hollings family becoming a part of my life, Katherine and John looming in my mind, and the sense of peace I now had about my mom's death and knowing that she was watching over me and had somehow brought these blessings to me to continue her legacy of teaching me life lessons.

I took the dream painting off the wall, not ready yet to call it finished. Propped back on the easel, I wanted to add just a few more details. As much as I didn't want to think about my dreams, when I painted I rarely had control over where my head went which is why it is so therapeutic for me. I could see Katherine, John, Becca, and even Gabriel in everything I painted. The barn started to take on new meaning for me as it reminded me of Pa's pain and how it had totally transformed him.

I took some time adding some details to the barn to make it appear more worn and weathered. It represented the hardships that Pa had been through, and a part of me hoped that by painting his barn with such care that I could somehow ease his guilt and allow him to see all the beauty that was around him, particularly his children. I was hopeful.

As much I wanted to deny these dreams, I went to bed with a sense of peace. I had to try and stop running from things in my life and embrace them. Could I do that? Could I really embrace how much my life had changed in the past year? I think I was starting to; as with my mom's death, there were just some things that can't be controlled or changed. I fell asleep with a smile on my lips and my mom in my thoughts.

The wind was rushing through my hair, the taste of pine on my lips. I was bareback on the most delicious creature, a beautiful black colt which was flying over the grass as if its feet were barely grasping the ground. It was the most freeing moment I probably ever had, and I let my body move as one with the horse. In the far distance, I could see the now familiar house and barn. Even farther away I could see a man working the fields with his horse and plow. It was a majestic, harmonious scene and brought me a beautiful sense of peace.

The horse began to slow as we approached the edge of the hill. Trotting to a stop, he lifted his head and shook it twice, his nostrils tasting the air. He snorted toward the ground as if to shake off a smell.

Starting off distant and unclear, a new sound was itching at our senses. It was a scream, someone yelling; I knew in an instant it was Becca. More screams added to the mix, and I knew they were in trouble. I kicked the horse as hard as I could, but it

wouldn't budge. I had to go find out what was happening.
Screaming at the animal to start moving, new panic rose up in
my throat choking off my screams. Far below me the screaming
grew louder, more intense, and as I scanned the horizon, my eyes
and nose found realization at the same moment. Smoke! Fire!
Fire! Smoke!

My ears rang with fear and panic. I couldn't get the
horse to move.

I woke up panting, sweat dripping in my eyes, hands
grabbing at the sheets. My eyes caught the clock; it was 3:30am. I
had to get back to sleep; the terror was rising in my chest. I had to
get to Becca and Katherine. I lay awake for a long time, hoping I
could go right back into the dream; I had to find out what was
happening, even though somewhere in the back of my mind, I felt
like I already knew, adding to the terror.

I shut my eyes and shut out the world, concentrating on my
breathing and willing myself to go back to sleep. My hands wound
around the sheets, my mind racing. A small, desperate sound
escaped my lips as my brain and sleep fought against each other.
Trying to calm myself was like trying to calm a raging hurricane as
it beat against the shore.

I desperately wanted get back to sleep so I could help
Katherine and Becca. My heart beat wildly in my chest. It was as
if sleep was mocking me from the next room, silently waiting for

my body to calm enough to sneak in. I tossed and turned and tried to get comfortable, but nothing seemed to work. In desperation I threw all the covers off, hoping that the cool breeze from the open window would soothe me back to sleep.

I don't remember the moment that sleep crept in, but I could smell the smoke before my body fully grabbed on to sleep.

Pushing through smoke, it was all I could see. I was running faster than I ever thought I could, and the house began to take shape in front of me. The fire and smoke were billowing out of the back of the house from the kitchen window. Pa, Ma, and Gabriel were running to the creek with buckets. Becca was seated under a tree screaming, her knees up to her chest.

From around the corner of the house, Katherine ran with an empty bucket. When she reached the front door, the bucket dropped out of her hands which flew to her gaping mouth. She stared at the front door, pulled her apron up over her mouth, and ran straight for the door. She flung the door open, creating the perfect opportunity for the flames in the back of the house to catch a deep breath. Once she crossed the doorway, smoke absorbed her shape.

Becca began screaming, "Katherine, Noooooo!" She was on her feet, bolting for the door. I reached her just as she reached full stride. Standing in front of her, I used everything inside of me to will her to sit back down, back up, not go running into the house, too. She bounded forward and knocked me square in the gut, sending her bouncing backward. She landed in a heap on the ground, staring right at me in astonishment. I didn't know if she saw me or could hear me, but I screamed, "Stay right there!" with as much authority as I could muster. She backed up and fell back on the ground, her mouth opened mid-scream.

I turned, expecting to see Katherine emerge from the flaming house. There was no sign of her, only the smoke and flames that now had taken over the front of the house. I raced for the door, knowing I had to do something. Inside, I couldn't see through the smoke, but I could tell instantly that it didn't affect my breathing; it was almost as if I were in a bubble moving through the smoke.

I strained my eyes to find her. Very faintly, above me, I heard coughing and knew instantly that she had gone up the ladder to rescue her letters. Just as I lunged for the ladder and began to pull myself up, someone grabbed me from behind and dragged me back out the door. My legs kicked out wildly in every direction, trying to make contact. I landed in a heap of petticoats and skirt on the dusty ground.

"We can't do anything to save her, Ava." I looked up into Jack's eyes as the tears began to stream. He was crying, too, and he gathered me into his arms and took me farther from the scene.

I clawed at him, beating his chest, clawing his face to let me go back to Katherine, back to drag her out of the house. My fingernails dug into his face; as I screamed at him, the tears streamed down my face. His arms grasped me tighter, not letting me go, and I knew the fight was futile. I was furious with him but buried my head in his chest and heaved uncontrollable sobs which took over my body, sending the whole scene shaking. Everything blurred with my tears.

The sobs were ringing in my ears as I struggled to free my face from the sheets that I was tangled in, pushing them away with my arms and legs flailing. Before realization completely took over, I was screaming for Jack. I bolted upright when my mind finally allowed me to realize I was no longer dreaming. The smell of smoke seemed to hang in my mind. I knew in the instant it took me to sit up that Katherine was dead, succumbed to the smoke and fire in a desperate attempt to rescue John's letters. I felt as if I had been punched in the stomach and tried to call out to her, only to have short breaths and sobs escape.

I knew what I had to do. It didn't require any thought on my part; for what seemed like the first time in my life my mind didn't have a decision to make, no more questions to be asked. The perfect, coherent thoughts were almost immediate.

I didn't even bother to change out of my Mickey Mouse pajamas. I was out the door and sprinting down the lane, the air heavy with fog. I didn't bother to knock when I got there, just threw open the door and ran for the steps. Almost running into Jack as he bounded to the bottom step, I threw my good arm around him, tears muting my voice.

Jack scooped me up in his arms and took me to the couch. I wiped at my tears and tried to find my voice.

Before I could, Jack softly said, "She's gone."

This brought a new round of tears which were joined by Jack's. After a few minutes the questions started.

"Did you know before tonight?" The sting of him knowing about Becca almost meeting a similar fate was still hanging on.

"No, not at all. I got there just as I saw you go into the house. I was so scared. I didn't know what could happen. I had never seen this dream before. Katherine had always been there."

"Why didn't you let me go to her?" I pushed against his chest as the memory flooded my mind.

"Ava, we can't mess around with these dreams, you wouldn't have been able to get to her anyway." My brows furrowed, showing him I didn't understand. "One time, many years ago, John fell off of the barn roof. I tried to go to him and lift him up, but it was like I was grabbing at a cloud."

"Then why was I able to push Becca back down to the ground?"

"I don't know. Besides, if you had been able to drag her outside, you would have been changing the course of her life."

"You don't know that Jack!" I yelled. "We don't even know that she is real." I shook my head, trying to make sense of what I was saying and feeling and completely contradicting myself.

The questions were swimming around my head like wind whipped leaves. These dreams had taken on a life of their own. I looked at Jack's face, full of anguish, and noticed two small scrapes on his face, just below his eye, obviously made by fingernails. I silently traced them with my fingertips as we stared at each other, not able to make sense of anything anymore.

"I don't care if you don't believe that John and Katherine were real, but I do. John is as real to me as I am myself."

I had nothing left to say, or that I wanted to say. A part of me was starting to believe him. I laid my head on Jack's shoulder, and that is how Elise found us at some point. I was vaguely aware that I was still in my pajamas, and I pushed Jack away gently, not entirely sure why I was slightly embarrassed.

"Is everything OK?" She looked at me in my pajamas and the bewildered look on Jack's face.

"I'm not sure, Mum." Jack looked at me with questioning eyes.

I took a deep breath, not wanting Jack to continue, to tell Elise about our dreams. I wasn't ready to share them with anyone else. Plus, in that quick moment, I knew what I had to do. I knew it with a certainty that I had never known before. It was as if Katherine and my mom were both reassuringly forcing me forward into this decision all along. Knowing that I was about to change the course of all of our lives, I blurted out, "I am staying at Rudyard Lake."

Elise was across the room, lifting me off the couch in a hug before I could take another breath. Over her shoulder I could see Jack's stunned face as he sat on the couch, hands folded in his lap, taking in what I had just said.

"Ava, that is wonderful news, I am so happy! I have to run and tell James. I will bring back some cinnamon buns for us to celebrate."

I watched Elise cross the kitchen and disappear into the store, wondering what I had just done. I didn't want to look at Jack, so I kept my eyes on the doorway waiting for something to break the silence.

"Do you mean it? You are really going to stay?" The puppy dog look in Jack's eyes made me giggle.

"Yes, Jack, I am staying. I don't know what these dreams mean, even if they are real. I know that you think that they are. But they taught me that I have to live my life and do what makes me happy. You make me happy, Jack. I don't want to regret a single thing; I am tired of loss and grief.

"Katherine taught me to live and to love. Pa's dramatic change because of his grief and how it affected his family showed me that life is too precious to waste a single moment of it, and I don't want to regret anything in my life. I have been fighting myself all summer to make sense of everything. Well, nothing makes sense to me, not my mother's death, these crazy dreams, my feelings for you and your family. I have been lying to myself, thinking that I can just leave it all behind. I don't want to end up like John and Katherine. I want to stay here and see where my life takes me.

By leaving here, I will also be leaving Katherine and John, Becca and Gabriel. I thought that I wanted to just run away from it all, but I have so many unanswered questions about their lives and I am not ready to let them go. It seems so crazy to say, but they have woven themselves into my life, and I don't think I can live without them. Or you. I love you, Jack."

"I love you too, my Ava."

Jack lifted me off the couch as his lips found mine, and finally I let go of everything and allowed our love to begin.

He whispered in my ear, "If you can wait and not be tired by waiting." I smiled recognizing the line from the poem. "I have been waiting for you all my life, Ava Banks. I knew it the first day I saw you struggling with those bags and that silly bike. I knew you were mine and I would just have to wait for you to realize it, too."

I didn't know what to say, but I knew that he was right, I had felt it that day, too, but wasn't ready to see it. I answered him with my lips, letting him know that he was mine, too.

Elsie, James, Jack, and I ate our cinnamon buns at the kitchen counter and discussed my plans, which I really hadn't thought through at all. James offered me a job at the market, on the spot. Elise was just overjoyed that I was staying, and we made plans to visit London and fix up my little cottage. I knew that I would have to talk to Aunt Cathy and Uncle Bern about staying here, but knowing them so well, I was sure they wouldn't put up much of a fuss. I finally allowed myself to be happier than I had been in months.

Jack and I walked hand in hand back to my cottage. I liked the sound of that- my cottage. It was so special and magical and felt truly like it belonged to me.

"So why the change all of a sudden? You were so angry yesterday, at me, at the dreams, everything."

"I am not sure, but I think seeing Katherine run back into those flames and knowing she wasn't going to get to be with John again, it just changed my view on my life.

"You know, I remember a conversation between the two men at the train station. They were talking about the double sunset and arguing about whether the sun had a second chance, like life. Does life gives you a chance to start again? Maybe this is my second chance?"

Rarely at a loss for words, Jack hugged me close.

We hung my paintings on the wall and talked about finding more spots around the lake for me to paint. At some point, Jack had moved my easel out to the edge of the lake and set up my paints and a fresh canvas. He settled himself on the mossy ground and motioned for me to begin.

I found my focal point, the little block of wooden planks out on the lake that Jack had fixed just six short weeks ago. So much had changed since then when all he was to me was an annoying, arrogant, impulsive boy. I began the painting while he watched me bring the lake to life.

"Make this one for Katherine," he said.

"No, this one is for you," I answered, as the beginnings of a canoe took shape.

Pa was alone in the barn writing a letter. Tears were streaming down his face as he wrote. I crouched down behind him, trying to read his scrawled letters, wanting so desperately to rest my hand on his shoulder.

Dear John,

It is with a heavy heart that I bring you this news. Katherine has passed on when a fire caught in the house. I am so sorry to have to tell you this as I know you were fond of each other. At one time we were family, and I know that I am to blame for what has happened between us.

Losing our Katherine made me realize how selfish I have been, and if I could go back and change everything that happened, beginning with your father's death, I would. I have behaved terribly since Peter's death, and I guess God has chosen to punish me by taking my Katherine.

I hope that one day you can forgive me.

In sorrow,

Albert

I woke with my mom's words on my lips, *"This, too, shall pass."* I never really gave this much thought until now. So much had changed, some good, some tragic. Change is difficult but unavoidable and was the theme of the past year of my life. I smiled as I began to fully grasp my mom's profound words and the full realization that I was now home.

Sometimes we have to change in order to move forward. I was so consumed with grief when my mom died that I didn't know how to live anymore. By coming to this magical place, I had found out how to live again and I knew that my mom was with me every step of the way. What part she played in the dreams, I don't know, but meeting Jack Hollings and having these strange dreams have helped me to fully realize what life is really all about and what my purpose is in it.

Fall was beautiful on the lake as the trees slowly turned golden. Reds and oranges dotted our surroundings as Jack slowly steered his boat, Katherine, out onto the lake. I was seated in front of him on the tiny captain's chair, my legs tucked up under me, as he stood behind me grasping the wheel, his arms protecting me on either side. I was wrapped in his hoodie slightly shaking from either the chill in the air or the lingering fear of actually being out on the lake. He kissed the top of my head and whispered in my ear, "I've got you, bug."

I looked around the lake at the colorful trees and green hills beyond, the small cottages dotting the shore and the birds swirling around overhead. I could just make out the faint twittering of a few of them calling to each other across the lake. My mind went to their conversation, and I knew exactly what they were saying, "Home, home, this is home."

I leaned in close to Jack and whispered in his ear, "This summer I will see that double sunset and it will mean so much more to me!"

"It is our sunset, yours, mine, Katherine and John's!"

As we came around the bend that led to my home, I could make out Aunt Cathy and Uncle Bern standing on shore, and we both raised our hands to wave. They waved back, and Uncle Bern put his arms around Aunt Cathy while they watched us ease the boat up to the dock. I couldn't help but smile at all the love that this lake had provided. It truly is a magical place, and I could only think that this magic had brought together Elise and James as well as Cathy and Bern so that Jack and I could eventually find each other again.

I wasn't sure what I believed about the dreams, if they are real or not. But, for whatever reason, these very real-like dreams came into my life and helped to change the way I looked at my life. I will never be able to explain the connection I felt with Katherine or how it is even possible that Jack and I were both experiencing the same dreams, but I do know that they brought us together in a way that would not have been possible otherwise.

The dreams still come, for both of us. There is never rhyme or reason to them. Becca and Gabriel are older now in some of the dreams and Katherine's presence is all around them. We don't dream about her much anymore. I think we had seen most of her life, but every once in a while, we get a glimpse of her. On rare occasions we get to see John and her together in happier times. Mostly we see John rebuilding his life. He and Albert work in the fields together now. John and Mary Alice have settled back into their home on the prairie, and life is how it should have been all along. Peter and Katherine are remembered often in our dreams. The hardest one to get through was when John returned home.

A lone horse was riding down the lane toward the burned out shell of the house. John slumped in the saddle, his emotions falling out before him. Jack and I sat motionless, powerless to move. His hands held mine, and as hard as I tried, I couldn't look away.

The wind whipped violently around the house as John dismounted at the door. No one else was in sight, just John and the charred ashes of Katherine's burial ground. John sank to the ground grabbing thick handfuls of mud as his tears fell.

Thankfully, Jack and I couldn't hear the sobs that wracked him, but his shoulders quivered violently. All we could hear was the wind howling which seemed to bring with it **the turbulence of John's emotions. Jack and I wordlessly let our tears fall, powerless to do anything else.**

P a g e | 207

I knew that Jack wanted to go to John and comfort him as he had done so many times before, for so many years. But even he couldn't make himself move. All we could do was watch the crumbling of a man so filled with grief. Eventually it was over, and the wind, mud, ashes, and sobs gave way to wakefulness.

Even though Jack and I had talked about it and knew it was coming, we were not prepared to be witnesses to the pain. Jack and I cried together, connecting in some deep, dark recess of our brains to the lost love story so long ago!

Pa's emotional turmoil at losing his daughter seemed to shift his mind back into focus. Over time we watched him slowly become a little more loving, a little less selfish. He began to heal, as we all did.

Epilogue

Jack and I traveled back to North Carolina in early November so that I could get a few of my things and Jack could experience his first American Thanksgiving. During our three week stay, Jack was able to get a glimpse into my life before Rudyard Lake. I was so glad that we had time with Aunt Cathy and Uncle Bern as well.

One morning Jack crept into my room and crawled under the covers with me, kissing my nose, my cheek, and my head until I slowly woke up with a smile.

"Have you noticed that we haven't dreamt about Katherine and John since we have been here?"

"I have."

"Do you find that odd?"

"I have tried not to think about it."

"I miss them."

"Me, too."

We cuddled together as the morning sun streamed in through the slats in the blinds. We didn't speak anymore about it but had a silent understanding that we needed to get back to the lake and to our dreams. I couldn't imagine my life without them, or Jack.

Aunt Cathy and Uncle Bern drove us to the airport. The chill of the early December morning surrounded us as we huddled outside the car saying our goodbyes. It would only be a few weeks before I would see them again as they were coming over for the holidays. This made me happier than I had ever been as I knew this holiday would be one of new beginnings with a new family.

"Don't forget to Skype us every Sunday." Aunt Cathy was so proud of her technological advances. "And I want pictures of the lake and the cottage, too."

"I will, I will, don't worry; it will be like I am not even gone. And I will see you in a few weeks anyway."

We all hugged and said our goodbyes, and Jack and I walked hand in hand into the airport. The flight was long, and I spent most of the flight dozing on Jack's shoulder. I was anxious to get back to the lake and the dreams that were waiting for us, along with our new life. At some point during the flight, I fell asleep on Jack's shoulder.

The plane started its decent, and I heard in my ear, "Wake up, bug, we are almost home."

My smile reached him before my eyes did.

"Home, that sounds so good! So I had a dream while I was sleeping."

"You did?" Jack's eyebrows shot up, asking the question I knew he was contemplating. "No, not of Katherine and John but of us."

"Well, tell me, silly."

Jack and I were seated in a canoe in the middle of the lake. His oars lay across his lap with a freshly painted boat on the paddle of one and a double sunset painted on the other. My oars lay on the bottom of the canoe, unused. On one paddle I had painted a train track which wound its way up the handle and connected to the track on the handle of the other oar. The track wound its way down the second oar to a train station on the paddle. The train was perched halfway down the handle of one of the oars. On the side of the train I had painted the numbers 1117. I still didn't know the significance of this number, but I knew it had been a large part of my summer, and it just seemed like the right thing to put on my oar.

Jack and I settled into the canoe, wrapped in each other's arms, waiting. In the distance we could see the sun just getting ready to set, the large peak right in its path.

"Here it goes, bug."

The sun slowly faded behind the peak, and we didn't take our eyes off of it. We sat in silence, watching, trying to witness every movement. I could feel Jack's heartbeat quicken against my back as I moved closer into him. He kissed the top of my head just as the sun faded behind the peak. The sun set for the first time. I turned my head to look at Jack, and our eyes were full of tears as we both remembered John and Katherine in that fading moment of the sun's first retreat.

Several moments later the first rays of the sun began to emerge on the other side of the peak. What would normally have been a simple act of nature now held such powerful meaning for us. My lips found his, and his breath enveloped me. Jack's hand found the back of my head, gently pressing me to him. I didn't want it to end; I didn't want to take my lips, my eyes off of him. But just like every sun, it must set. As I slowly pulled away from his mouth, the sun was blazing fully on the other side of the peak. We watched it live again for a few moments, blazing brightly across the lake. Those moments were the happiest of my life. Everything was exactly as it was supposed to be.

"Grab your oars; we always leave before it sets again."

Even though I didn't want this moment to end, I knew it wasn't really an ending, but a beginning of many more moments to come. I also knew, without him saying it, that this is why we were going to leave before the second setting of the sun.

I carefully maneuvered myself and my oars to the other end of the canoe, marveling at my confidence near the water now. Jack and I slowly rowed the canoe back to the cottage in silence, not watching the sun make its final decent behind the hill. I breathed in the warm England air and smiled at Jack's happy face as the canoe stuttered across the rocky bottom of the shoreline.

When I was finished telling Jack about the dream, I looked into his eyes, seeing them glisten with unshed tears. He kissed my nose uttering, "That was the most beautiful dream yet."

Elise and James could barely contain their excitement as they greeted us at the car, anxious to take us home. Jack talked the entire ride back to the cottage, telling them all about every detail of our trip. Elise and I caught each other's eye in the rear view mirror and smiled at each other until I had to turn away, stifling a giggle. I don't think I had ever seen Jack so animated, and that was saying a lot.

That night, Jack and I decided to sleep on the couches together at his house, and we fell asleep, like we had so many months before, looking at each other across the silence.

The sounds of laughter rang in my ears even before my mind had fully grasped sleep. I followed the sound until I was standing in the middle of Becca's garden, almost trampling down a few flowers. I gingerly stepped out of the garden and followed the sound of laughter to the meadow behind the barn. There I found Ma, Pa, Gabe, Becca, John and Mary Alice enjoying a picnic lunch.

Gabriel was trailing a stick through the muddy banks of the river while Pa and Becca chased after each other, the source of the laughter. The transformation of all of them warmed my heart. Becca was a little bit taller and had filled out a bit. Gabe was almost as tall as John and no longer held that little boy sour face. John was sitting next to his mother, working with some wood. When I walked over to him, I saw that he was making two grave markers. The one on the ground read, "Peter John Cooper 6-12-1802 to 9-22-1840 Husband, Father and Friend." The other one in his hand read "Katherine Ava Adkins 11-17-1827-10-10-1845 Daughter, Sister and Friend." John was adding small hearts in the corner, edging out the shapes with his knife. Her birthday, 11-17, was that number I had been seeing all summer.

I tried to cover my mouth with my hand as I also took in her full name but found that it was entwined in Jack's hand. He was also looking at her name and gave me a wink. I wanted to tell him about her birth date and was overcome with emotion over the connection to her name, but I couldn't because standing right in front of us was Becca.

She was staring at us, everyone else oblivious to her halt in laughter and play. Her hair was blowing lightly in the wind. Her eyes were big and seemed to look at us, yet right through us at the same time. She reached out to touch our entwined fingers. I felt a faint wisp of wind across my knuckles as little Becca whispered, "Katherine."

I woke in Jack's arms, his lips pressing sweet kisses in my hair. I could tell he was smiling, and as I leaned up to kiss him, so was I. There will be pain, there will be suffering, loss, and grief, but there will always be another chance for smiles, too. Life always seems to have a way of bringing us back to where we belong, making everything right again, after all the lessons are learned.

Acknowledgements

This book would not have been written without the support of so many people. Sandra Rossi you were the first to know about this crazy adventure and had I listened to you Ava and Jack would be zombie apocalypse fighting vampires. Thank you for always being there for me and for giving Ava her name.

Deep gratitude to Russ Jones for giving me the early encouragement to keep writing and for giving me invaluable feedback on the beginnings of the story.

Shannon Smith, my enthusiastic cheerleader, thank you for being my first reader and giving Ava and Jack your sign of approval. Jen Kuessner and Jen Bethke, your insight from a reader's prospective gave me exactly what I needed to put the finishing touches on the story and finally finish revising.

Special thanks and admiration to my sister, Amy Bittner, who took the time to edit my story, you are forevermore the comma queen.

Immeasurable love for my mom and dad, Dell and Otts Smith, and my amazing daughters, Anna and Grace, for believing in me and loving me unconditionally. Mom-Mom you were with me every step of the way and every time I see 1117, I know you are watching over me.

Thanks to my bestie, Staci Vogt, who knows I am crazy and loves me anyway and to all of my friends who love me and supported me on this journey.

Google maps thank you for the many hours of stalking you have provided me. If I were not bored and stalking lakes in England I may not have ever written this book. Special thanks to Rudyard Lake, UK for being the backdrop and motivation for Ava and Jack's adventures. To my English pal, Sue Powley, thank you for your input on all things British!

I would like to thank the musicians that saw me through many many hours of writing. One Republic, Lifehouse, James Morrison and Rascal Flatts, thank you for keeping me company and providing just the right musical inspiration for my writing.

Special thanks to my main musical muse, Gavin Degraw. Your lyrics and music mean so much to me and kept me company through hours of edits and revisions. Being a fan of your music has also brought some pretty amazing friends into my life. Keep doing what you're doing Music Man.

Vickie Wasserman, this story would not have been written if it weren't for your belief in me. Thank you for showing me that there is light on the other side and sometimes that "place over there" is really right in front of me.

About the Author

I am an elementary technology teacher by profession and a single mom of two amazing daughters, Anna and Grace. Maryland has always been my home. Writing was something I did growing up but lost the love of it in the midst of raising children and working. Sometimes life changes you and in the midst of some pretty crazy times I began to write again, as a hobby. A year and a half later this story was written. Writing it was something I did just for me but somewhere along the way I decided I wanted to share it with others. With an affinity for the English language but little else in my writing tool box I began this adventure.

When I am not working or raising children you can probably find me reading on my front porch. My love of reading is what ultimately led me to become a writer. My happy place would be on a grand porch over-looking a serene lake with mountains in the distance, as long as there is wifi for my cell phone and laptop that I would be doomed without.